T. J. GREEN

TOM'S INHERITANCE

YOUNG ADULT ARTHURIAN FANTASY

Tom's Inheritance

Published by Mountolive Publishing

2nd Edition January 2017

ISBN 978-0-473-38679-5

For Jason

"Or how should England dreaming of *his* sons
Hope more for these than some inheritance
Of such a life, a heart, a mind as thine"

– Alfred, Lord Tennyson (1809–92)

Idylls of the King

Other Titles by TJ Green

Tom's Arthurian Legacy Series

Twice Born

Galatine's Curse

Tom's Arthurian Legacy Box Set

White Haven Witches Series

Buried Magic

Magic Unbound

Magic Unleashed

Invite from the author -

You can get two free short stories, Excalibur Rises and Jack's Encounter, by subscribing to my newsletter. You will also receive free character sheets of all the main Whitehaven Witches.

Details can be found at the end of Tom's Inheritance.

.

Prologue

One evening towards the end of summer, Jack strolled down the path to the bottom of his garden, pushing through the thick vegetation that crowded on either side. The air was thick with pollen and heat, and bees buzzed drunkenly around him. He rested his elbows on the gate and leant his weight against it, feeling his pruning clippers push into his hip. He lit his pipe, narrowing his eyes against the smoke, which he blew around him in an effort to drive off the midges that now appeared in the twilight.

Beyond the gate a stream trickled by, and here the air was cooler. It smelt earthy and damp; he could feel its sharpness on the back of his throat.

Jack's knees and lower back ached. He'd spent too long in the garden and he was too old to cope with it as he used to. He rubbed his cheek and felt the stubble. He could almost feel the grey in it, as if it were coarser than in his youth.

The silence was disturbed only by the stream, and the wind easing through the trees. He breathed deeply, savouring the cool and the smoke. Shadows slanting through the trees cast the banks into deep shadow, so that he could no longer distinguish between the trees, the banks, the rocks or the stream.

He started singing an old folk tune, and as he did, saw something stir at the foot of the gnarled yew tree across the stream. Were his eyes playing tricks on him? It looked as if a figure was moving, as if someone was stirring from a long deep sleep. Maybe what looked like long limbs were in fact tree roots thrown into relief by the shadows, and what looked like a face was a knot in the trunk. But then the figure moved again, and legs and arms became distinct. With a jolt, he realised he was looking into two unblinking eyes, fixed upon him with an unexpected intensity.

Jack's singing faltered and he blinked rapidly, several times. The figure moved its head as if it were a snake, its eyes glittering, before blinking languorously. It rose in one swift movement and became a man. No, not a man, but something that looked like a man; tall and slim with the grace of wind through tall grass, or water over stones. He was dressed in shades of green and a long cloak fell from his shoulders, almost to his feet, shimmering like a low mist.

And Jack knew what it must be, and that all the stories from his childhood were true.

1 The Visitors

A flicker of movement in the wood caught Tom's attention. Normally he would take no notice; people often walked in the wood. But this time something was different. The dark shapes flitting around the trees seemed to be hiding, and for the briefest of seconds he saw a tall figure stepping back between the trees before it vanished.

He stood in his grandfather's kitchen, looking through the broad window that framed the garden, down to the wood beyond. What if this strange activity in the wood was to do with Granddad?

More than a year ago, when Tom was fourteen, his grandfather, Jack, had mysteriously disappeared. He'd walked out of his house one evening and never came back. There was no sign of a struggle, only a note left for the family, explaining that he was going on trip with a new friend and that he would send a "sign" that he was all right.

Impatient after months of waiting, Tom grabbed his jacket and headed into the garden. He jogged down the path, through the gate and across the stream, cursing under his breath as he plunged into an icy pool. He thrust onwards, pushing aside the overhanging branches of a yew before pausing to look around.

The wood was still and silent. Tom edged forward, peering behind tree trunks and up into the bare branches high overhead. A prickle of unease travelled up his spine and he spun around, convinced he was being watched. Frustrated, he yelled, "Who's there? I know someone's there. I saw you!"

The wood remained silent, frozen in watchfulness, and he stepped back nervously, a branch cracking loudly beneath his feet like a gunshot.

Swallowing his fear he shouted again. "I know you can hear me! Come out!"

His prickle of unease grew stronger, and feeling suddenly alone and defenceless, he became sharply aware of the biting cold and his freezing feet. Time to go. Unwilling to turn his back on whatever was out there, he walked slowly backwards, scanning left and right until he reached the stream.

Someone or something was out there; he knew it, but there was nothing more he could do. Reluctantly, he returned to the cottage.

The heating was turned up high, but the kitchen still felt cold. Tom sank into the comfortable overstuffed armchair next to the big stone fireplace and pulled off his boots and socks, placing them on the hearth. He lit the fire, and as the flames caught and raced along the wood, he stood warming himself, absentmindedly running his hands through his dark blond hair. Although the prickle along his spine had gone, the after-effects remained and he felt strangely unsettled, as if his privacy had been invaded.

Tom glanced around the kitchen, reassuring himself with its solid familiarity. A few months ago, he and his father had moved into the cottage, which had stood empty since Granddad's disappearance. A terrible fight between his parents had prompted the move. Dad had walked out, saying he was going to "look after" the cottage. Tom had come with him, while his little sister had stayed with Mum. But the house felt different without Granddad in it, and Tom missed him. Dad was distracted and working long hours, and every now and again there were more arguments between his parents over the phone.

Tom's gaze drifted to one end of the mantelpiece, to a blue stripy bowl filled with old keys, nails and screws. Beneath it was Granddad's last letter. He picked it up and read it again, musing that he had never known Granddad go on a trip – he'd always been here at the cottage, tending his garden and smoking his pipe. But Dad said he used to travel a lot when he was younger. Maybe he'd got bored and wanted a change.

As he stood reading and warming his feet, he heard the front door open and a voice called out, "Hiya, it's me. Where are you?"

"I'm in the kitchen."

The door pushed open and a small slim girl came in, strawberry blond hair swinging behind her. It was his fourteen-year-old cousin, Rebecca, also known as Beansprout on account of her lean and lanky frame. "What you up to?"

"Not much, just looking at Granddad's letter again. What *you* up to?"

She rolled her eyes. "Mum's driving me mad, fussing about food and stuff for Christmas. I'm heading to the shop to pick up some extras and thought I'd drop in." She noticed his wet boots. "Where have you been?"

He paused, wondering how much to say, then grinned. "Hunting!"

She frowned, "Hunting what?"

"Watchers in the woods."

"Have you gone mad? What are you on about?" She moved to the window and looked out. "There's no-one there."

He joined her, still carrying his granddad's letter. "But there was. Someone was over there, watching this house."

She noticed the letter in Tom's hand. "Why are you reading Granddad's letter again? Do you know where he's gone?"

Tom sighed. "No, I've told you before. I have no idea."

"So why are you looking at his letter again?"

"Because I think that whoever's watching, knows something about Granddad."

"That seems a bit of a leap Tom!" she said, looking doubtful. "Did you find anyone?"

"No." He gazed out of the window, desperately hoping he'd see something again. "But I swear someone was there, watching me. I could feel it."

Suddenly excited she said, "Let's go again. Two of us may have more luck."

Tom shook his head. "What's the point? What would we say? 'Have you kidnapped my granddad?' They'd laugh at us."

"But if we find them, we can follow them and see where they go."

"Now who's being mad? We'd be spotted!"

She grabbed the letter off him, "Maybe they're here to leave the sign!"

Beansprout's excitement was catching and he grinned. "Maybe. We might solve the mystery!"

Beansprout leaned against the counter and looked around the kitchen. "It's weird, isn't it? Why would he just leave and not tell us where he was going?"

"OK," he said, "it's too late today, but we'll go out there again tomorrow and have another look. We'll go a bit further, maybe up to the folly, see if we can see anything. If you want to come?"

"Of course I want to come. Anything to get out of Christmas prep," she said with a huff. "I'll bring food too. What time?"

"About nine?" Tom thought the earlier they went, the more time they'd have. Dad would be at work, so no one would worry about where they were.

"Great, I'll be here. Anyway I better get on. Need anything?"

"Nah, I'm good," he said, with a shrug. "See you tomorrow. And don't be late."

2 A Sign

The next morning was bright and clear, and Tom woke early, jolting out of an unsatisfactory night's sleep. Ever since Granddad had disappeared he'd been having strange dreams about a woman with long white hair. She whispered his name to him. "Tom," she called, "it is time." But she never said anything else, and when he tried to answer she would fade away and the dream would evaporate.

Sometimes other images would come. He would see water, and the glint of something shining deep down beneath the shifting waves where he couldn't see it clearly. Sometimes he saw a bright blaze of firelight, and heard a low murmured chanting that became louder and louder until it roared in his ears before receding like a tide. And sometimes when he woke up, it felt like someone had punched him on the birthmark at the top of his arm.

Shrugging off the dreams which he had long since decided to ignore, he lay in bed, looking forward to the day that stretched before him, wondering what it might hold. He'd already packed his backpack with spare socks, a jumper and bottles of water, and the sandwiches he'd made the night before – ham and cheese – were waiting in the fridge.

He had no idea what he might find today, or even what to look for, but it would be good to have company. Beansprout was right, he'd been moody lately. But he couldn't help it; everything had changed.

He jumped out of bed and went to look at an old map on the bedroom wall. It showed the surrounding land as it had been over a hundred years ago. The cottages along the stream, including Granddad's, were marked, but the fields and farmland behind them were now covered in houses. The large woods across the narrow stream remained unchanged and were still surrounded by fields, and just visible at the top edge of the map was the small village of Downtree, also virtually unchanged since the map had been made.

Marked on the map, in the centre of the wood, was the strange, tumbledown stone tower that he and Beansprout would walk to today. Mishap Folly had been built more than a hundred years ago by the owner of the manor house. It was so-called because of the series of unfortunate events that had overtaken the owner: the manor had been damaged by fire, crops had failed, and the owner's son had died after been thrown from a horse. Then the owner himself had disappeared and was never seen again.

The tower had stood empty over the years, beginning to crumble as the woods encroached on all sides.

Tom estimated it would take an hour or so to walk there. It was probably unlikely that Granddad had passed that way, but it had always annoyed Tom that so far, no one had checked it out.

He dragged on his jeans, pulled on a T-shirt and jumper, and ran down the stairs. After putting some bread in the toaster he opened the back door and took a deep breath as the cold crisp air came flooding in. As he stepped outside he noticed an odd-shaped package on the doorstep. How had that got there?

He grabbed the parcel as if it might suddenly disappear, and turned back into the kitchen to examine it.

The outer wrapping was a lightweight piece of bark, and as he lifted the edges a gauzy material shimmered beneath it. He unfolded it to find his grandfather's watch and a note. Tom gasped. Who had brought this?

Behind him the toaster popped loudly and in shock he dropped everything onto the table. Cross with himself for being so jumpy, he frowned at the toaster as he pulled the note from under the watch. It was Granddad's writing.

Sorry for the delay, but I've been very busy!
I've sent you my watch as it doesn't really work here, but I wanted you to know that I'm all right.
I probably won't be coming home so I hope someone's looking after the house and garden.
I miss you all, but I know you'll be fine.
Don't try to find me!
Love, Granddad xxx

Tom felt hugely relieved to know Granddad was fine. And then he felt really cross. What did he mean, "Don't try to find me"? How ridiculous. Where on Earth was he?

The letter was written on thick parchment-like paper. He wondered if there was some sort of secret message in it, but after reading the note several times, was sure there wasn't.

He kicked the table in frustration and buttered his now cold toast. Beansprout had better be on time. Whoever had delivered the note might still be around, and Tom intended to find them.

Beansprout was as mystified as Tom. She propped her

bulging backpack against the table and examined the package while Tom finished his breakfast.

"Who brings a watch wrapped in bark, Tom? That's just odd. Perhaps he's run out of money and is living off the land, like Robinson Crusoe?"

"And his Man Friday has brought us a present? I doubt it. Besides, he said he doesn't need his watch where he is, so he must be somewhere else!"

"Where else? That doesn't make sense either."

"None of this makes sense Beansprout!" Beansprout glared at him, but changed the subject. "So are we going to leave your dad a message?"

"What did you tell your mum?"

"Just that we're going out for the day and I'd see her this evening."

"Cool, I'll do the same."

He scribbled a note and left it on the kitchen table, then put the contents of the package in his backpack.

The wood was a tangled mass of bare tree limbs, its floor carpeted in dead leaves. Branches sprang at them, catching their hair and scratching their faces. They slipped and slid on the damp ground, stubbing their toes against roots that lay hidden under layers of slimy leaves.

Spooked by the stillness around them, which seemed to mock their attempts at conversation, they fell silent; the only sound was their ragged breathing and the occasional crack of a twig.

It wasn't until he spotted the roof of the folly through the trees that Tom broke the silence. "I can see it, we're nearly there!"

They emerged into a clearing. The round tower

loomed above them, its stone walls cracked and crumbling, its roof jagged. The ground was littered with broken stones. Moss had spread like patchwork, and ivy snaked up the walls until there was barely an inch of grey stone to see.

"Wow!" said Beansprout, "I didn't know it was so big!"

"You check the inside and I'll look round the back," Tom said. "Be careful!" he added as he tripped over a snaking branch of ivy.

"Yeah, yeah," he heard her mutter as she made her way to the entrance. "I'm not a child!"

Tom reached the far side of the tower. He peered around him at the trees, the tower, and the debris on the floor, and all at once felt stupid. What was he thinking? That he could find Granddad, or the person who had brought the package? He huffed, and thumped back against the wall before sliding to the floor, his backpack squashed behind him.

Without a whisper of noise, a tall figure emerged from the wood and walked towards him, stopping a few feet away. It was a young man, just a few years older than Tom, with long dark hair and pale skin. There was something different about him that Tom couldn't quite put his finger on. He wore a loose pale-grey shirt and black cotton trousers tucked into leather boots. A long, thick, grey cloak hung from his shoulders, almost reaching the ground. But what was unnerving was the sword at his side, and the longbow and arrows visible over his shoulder.

For a while they assessed each other, before the man dropped to the ground and sat cross-legged.

"Greetings," he said. "My name is Woodsmoke." His voice was soft and low with a strange accent.

Surprised, Tom said, "Hi."

"And you are?"

After debating whether telling this stranger anything was a good idea, he said, "Tom."

Woodsmoke nodded, as if that was the answer he'd been expecting. "I know your grandfather," he said.

Tom's head shot forward, his mouth open wide. "How? Have you seen him recently? Is he all right?"

Woodsmoke laughed, so gently it sounded like rain on the roof. "So many questions, Tom. You remind me of him. He's fine. He doesn't want you to worry about him. That's why I brought his watch for you."

"It was you? And you were in the wood yesterday! But where is he? I want to see him. So much has happened since he left, he could help – I know he could."

"He's too far away to help, Tom. As he said in his letter, he won't be coming back. Whatever it is, you'll have to manage. You aren't alone, are you?" Woodsmoke looked concerned, as if he'd misunderstood.

"No, I live with my dad. But ..." He shrugged.

Woodsmoke sighed. "I don't know if he could help, Tom."

"Well, I want to see him anyway!"

"I'm sorry, that's not possible. I shouldn't be speaking to you, I should have just gone." Woodsmoke looked cross with himself. "I must go now, I have a long way to travel, and you must go home too. Stop worrying, your grandfather is fine." He rose swiftly to his feet, but as he turned to go, a woman came running around the side of the tower.

"Woodsmoke, quickly – the girl has gone into the tunnel."

"You said you'd sealed it!"

By now Tom was on his feet and looking at both of them. "What girl? Do you mean Beansprout?" But Woodsmoke and the woman were already running back round the tower.

3 Into the Other

Tom hurtled after them, trying not to fall and break his neck, and saw Woodsmoke and the woman disappear into a hole in the ground he was sure hadn't been there before. Looking around the clearing he saw no sign of Beansprout, so he threw himself into the hole after them.

For several seconds he slid and coughed as dust rose in waves around him. Then he stopped with a thump, and looked up to find himself in a tunnel. Woodsmoke was looking at him in exasperation.

"You should not be here!"

"I'm coming with you if Beansprout's down here. She's my cousin; I'm not leaving without her." All thoughts of his grandfather were temporarily forgotten.

Before Woodsmoke could answer, the woman shouted, "Come on!"

Woodsmoke pulled Tom to his feet, saying, "Stay close." He looked above Tom's head, murmuring something under his breath that Tom couldn't understand, then a door slid shut across the opening. Tom experienced a moment of panic as he realised he was trapped, but before he could say anything, Woodsmoke set off after the woman.

Tom followed. The tunnel was narrow and dark, lit by occasional burning torches attached to the wall, their flames giving off an acrid smoke that made Tom's eyes smart. The roof was low and the walls rough, tree roots spearing in from all directions.

Woodsmoke moved ahead with ease, gliding through the gaps. They reached an archway made of smooth, close-fitting stone, across the top of which words were carved in a strange language.

Woodsmoke shouted, "Brenna, wait!"

The woman called back, her voice flattened by the earth above them. "Hurry up!"

On the other side of the arch, the tunnel walls were made of the same smooth grey stone, the ceiling rising higher and higher as the walls moved further apart. The path sloped downwards, deeper and deeper into the earth.

Tom couldn't understand how the woman had got ahead of them so quickly, but as they rounded the corner he saw her standing in the middle of a high domed space. Brenna had the whitest skin he'd ever seen, but her hair, falling long and straight to the base of her back, was so black that it had glints of blue in it. In contrast to her skin, her eyes were dark, the whites barely visible. Like Woodsmoke, she carried a sword at her belt. She looked completely at home in this space. It seemed to fold around her.

The floor was laid with intricately carved stones forming patterns of diamonds, circles, and interlocking squares, while the walls were decorated with patterns of leaves and animals – fierce-looking winged creatures with hooves and fangs. Tom thought he could hear murmurings and rustlings.

Around the edge of the semi-circular cavern were four wide-arched entranceways. Beyond each was a black void; it was as if the floor just dropped away. Beansprout was nowhere in sight.

"Where is she? Did you see where she went?"

Tom was worried by the urgency in Woodsmoke's voice. However, Brenna looked calm.

"She went into the Realm of Water," she replied.

Woodsmoke turned to Tom. "You must wait here; you cannot come with us."

Tom looked around at this strange place so far beneath the earth, and knew he must go too. They didn't know Beansprout – they would need his help to find her. And besides, what if something came out of those arches? What if Woodsmoke and Brenna never came back? He would die down here, entombed.

"No," he said. "I'm coming. You can bring us both back." In those seconds Tom felt the weight of the backpack on his shoulders and tasted the decay in the air around him, and knew he was watched by all those hundreds of eyes in the carvings as they waited with him in the long-abandoned tunnel.

Woodsmoke swore under his breath and then extended one hand to Tom and the other to Brenna. She turned and quickly pulled them into one of the archways.

For several seconds Tom felt completely weightless, and couldn't tell if he was falling or flying, or simply suspended in the dark, a speck in an ocean of blackness. He heard a murmur, like waves lapping a beach, and a whispered "Welcome," then felt a wrenching pull in the centre of his body. All at once there was light and ground beneath his feet. He felt himself cry out as air was forced from his body, and his hands instinctively reached out to protect himself as he pitched forward onto a mixture of hard grey rock and moss.

Taking a deep breath he pushed back onto his haunches and looked around. They were on a broad stone path in the centre of a large horseshoe-shaped curve of rock and water. Granite cliffs stretched high into the air, and waterfalls streamed down from the misty heights into an enormous lake in front of them, frothing and churning where they hit the water. The cliffs were pitted with caves and crevasses, some small, others cathedral-like in their enormity. Ferns grew everywhere, anchored to the rock with clinging roots. A broad stone bridge crossed to the far side of the lake, and beyond that the cliffs extended in a straight line, a deep gorge disappearing into the distance.

And it was hot and humid. Despite the fact that the sun was sinking in a cloudless pale blue sky, the oppressive heat lay across them like a blanket, and sweat was already beading on Tom's brow.

Woodsmoke and Brenna seemed nervous. "It brought us here? To the Eye? Of all the places ..." Woodsmoke whispered.

Brenna's pallor was almost luminous in this light, which made her eyes appear even darker. "Well we must be quick then – and quiet!" she said.

Tom wanted to ask where they were, and what the Eye was, and who had whispered in his head so quietly it was as if he'd imagined it, but Brenna's words stilled his tongue.

They hurried across the bridge. It wasn't until he was halfway across that Tom thought to look below him, into the clear green water, and he stopped, astonished. Beneath the waves was a huge castle with turrets, parapets, courtyards and towers. It was completely intact; it wasn't a ruin that had been swallowed by the lake. Far below he saw lights flashing in the darkness on the floor of the lake, and wondered who lived there. He ran to catch up to Woodsmoke, pulling at his arm. Woodsmoke hissed, "Wait".

The bridge ended with a low parapet, and they gazed over its edge. Water from the lake thundered to the base of the gorge to form a fast-flowing river. He saw a figure down there, much further along on the right.

"Look – out there. Is that Beansprout? Why is she down there?" he asked, bewildered.

"The doorways open onto different spaces, depending on the time you enter," said Brenna. "The closer you are in time when you cross, the closer in distance you will be. That's why we had to come here quickly,"

"We have to get down there. She must be terrified!"

Brenna looked at Woodsmoke. "I'll go first, I can wait with her. We'll walk back this way." Then, in front of Tom's eyes, she turned into a big black bird and plunged over the parapet, heading towards Beansprout.

Astonished, Tom turned to Woodsmoke. "What is this place? Where am I?"

"You're in the Eye, which is the centre of The Realm of Water. It can be dangerous, so we need to leave. Stay quiet."

Woodsmoke led the way down a wide stone ramp that dropped to the floor of the gorge. The cliffs either side were so high that Tom felt the size of an ant. It seemed to take forever to cross a small distance, as if they were crawling. It didn't help that he kept slowing down to look around him. He wanted to see everything, to imprint it on his mind forever.

On the far side of the gorge was an identical ramp; the gorge was in symmetry. He wondered who had designed it all. It was peaceful and beautiful.

"We haven't got all day, Tom. Hurry up." Woodsmoke's strides were long and fluid, and Tom almost had to jog to keep up with him.

"Is this where you live?"

"No, I live in the Realm of Earth, which is where your granddad is."

Woodsmoke kept his voice low and Tom struggled to hear him.

"Is that close? Are we going there next?"

"No. You are going home next. And keep close to the cliff side; we'll be less visible there."

Tom decided to ignore the "going home" warning and asked, "Why is it sometimes dangerous here?"

"The water spirits who live here are not always friendly, and there are other things lurking in the rocks and the water that are even more frightening. It is not good that it's so late in the day." He looked thoughtfully at Tom and asked, "Why is it that a girl would go into a tunnel she doesn't know, and then enter an archway that is black and appears to lead nowhere? Is she stupid?"

It was a good question. Tom wasn't sure how to answer, but he thought he should defend Beansprout because he was actually pleased to be here.

"She's quite inquisitive," was all he could think of.

"Really?"

Tom thought he detected sarcasm. "I suppose she thought she was helping. She probably thought our grandfather was living in the tunnel beneath the folly."

"Really?" Woodsmoke said again.

"Well, I would have thought so if I'd seen the tunnel; I'd have done the same thing. Anyway, it's your fault. You left the tunnel open."

Woodsmoke's eyes narrowed as he stared at Tom. "Actually, Brenna did."

Tom realised he'd better not be cheeky, or Woodsmoke might leave him here.

It was nearly dark when they reached the others. Brenna and Beansprout were waiting inside a small cleft in the rock face.

"Tom!" Beansprout said nervously. "Sorry to have caused so much trouble." She looked as if she was going to hug him, but thought better of it.

"Are you OK?" he asked.

"I am now." She smiled at Brenna. "I was a bit panic-stricken at first."

"Well, this is Woodsmoke and he's annoyed! Woodsmoke, my cousin Beansprout."

Woodsmoke nodded briefly, and then said, "We need to get out of here." He turned to Brenna. "I think we should go higher, find a cave and get out of sight."

"I've already found one." Brenna pointed to a small black hole in the rock wall, several metres above the path. "It's small, but there are no other caves leading off it. It's the best we can do for now."

Woodsmoke sighed. "All right. Lead the way."

4 The Eye

Excitement and nervousness fought inside Tom's head. He wanted to see more of the Eye and the Realm of Water, but he didn't want to come across the weird and dangerous creatures that lurked beneath the waters. Well, actually he *did* want to see them, but from a safe distance.

The four of them were at the back of a shallow cave looking out over the gorge. It was hot and airless, and Tom was uncomfortably sweaty. He could just see Woodsmoke and Brenna in the darkness as they leaned back against the walls, seemingly deep in thought.

"So what's the plan?" he asked.

"We need to find another portal, Tom," said Woodsmoke, "so we can take you back home. The portals between the four worlds are rarely used now. We certainly don't know where to find one here, so we'll need to search, but we can't do that at night." He groaned and rubbed his hands across his face. "It could take us days. And if we can't find a portal it will be a long journey back to our realm."

Beansprout spoke, her voice quiet. "I'm sorry. It's my fault we're here. I didn't mean to ..." Her voice trailed off with a sigh.

Tom asked, "What happened? How ...?"

"I was eating and I saw this hole in the ground, so I thought I should check it out – you know, just in case. So I stuck my head in and then ended up sliding in. Once I was in

28

I thought I'd see where it went."

"But why didn't you call me when you saw it?"

Beansprout shrugged. "In case it was nothing. I followed that tunnel, which was really amazing, and then I sort of stuck my hand in that black hole and it pulled me right in!" She sounded sheepish and delighted with herself all at the same time. "I freaked out initially, kind of froze, then decided I should sit tight and hope someone came for me – and here you are!"

Woodsmoke sounded cross. "Well, you are very lucky we found you intact. In fact you are lucky we found you at all."

The word "intact" seemed to hang in the air.

"Well I'm starved," said Beansprout. "Let's eat."

"Great idea," Tom answered. "And while we eat you can tell us about this place, and how you know our granddad."

Beansprout and Tom rummaged through their backpacks, handing out food and drinks.

"Very well," said Woodsmoke. He paused, as if wondering how much to tell them. "First you need to know we are no longer in your world. I'm sure that's obvious. We are in the Otherworld, which lies alongside yours. There are four realms here – Earth, Air, Water and Fire – and different spirits and beings live in each. This, as you know, is the Realm of Water, and we have arrived in the Eye, the absolute centre of the realm, where the Emperor lives. Brenna and I are from the Realm of Earth. Years ago we passed between the four realms all the time, but for years now we have remained separate. It's the same with your world – we no longer come and go from there as we used to. In your world we have different names – faeries, elves, fauns, nymphs, or even Sidhe."

"Faeries!" gasped Beansprout. "Like in the old stories – the ones where people would disappear and never be seen again?"

"That's right. At certain times of day – dawn and dusk – and in certain places, the edges of our worlds would dissolve and humans could pass from their world to ours, usually by accident. Now, for most people, only the portals will enable passage, but they are well hidden."

"Hidden how? By magic?" asked Tom.

"Of a sort. And they are usually built underground, or in remote places, with concealed entrances. My grandfather, Fahey, was trapped in your world for many years. When he was released from the spell, he managed to find the portals in the wood. He said he could hear our realm singing to him, as if to call him home, and he followed the music."

"Where was he trapped?" asked Beansprout.

"In that old yew tree at the edge of the wood beyond your grandfather's garden. He was trying to travel to Avalon but triggered a spell. For years we had no idea what had happened to him, although we searched and searched." He shook his head. "And then he returned a few months ago, with your grandfather, Jack. He was the first person Fahey saw after he was released from the spell."

"Wow!" Tom exclaimed, "So why is Granddad here?"

"My grandfather liked him and so he invited him. I don't know why he said yes, Tom. I know how much I missed my grandfather – that's why I agreed to bring you that package, so you wouldn't worry."

"Then you must know why we want to see him, Woodsmoke."

"I do, but it's not that easy. Our world is dangerous,

full of magic, strange places and even stranger creatures; far more dangerous than your world is to us. I have heard rumours of the Emperor here. If they are true, he's someone we should keep away from."

"So if this is the Realm of Water, why are we on land?" Beansprout asked.

"A portion of it *is* land, although it's filled with rivers and waterways. Most of the realm is under the sea; whole cities are sprawled across the sea bed, or perched on underwater mountain ranges or deep within trenches far from light. From what I have heard there are different groups who all fight for control, and petty skirmishes are constantly breaking out. The Emperor must be a busy man," Woodsmoke said thoughtfully.

"Do people fight in the Realm of Earth too?" Tom asked.

"Sometimes. There are disturbing rumours coming out of Aeriken Forest in our realm. The Queen of the Aerikeen is strange, and rarely seen. Her people have disappeared from the villages." He exchanged a worried glance with Brenna. "We fear something terrible is happening there."

"Do you know Jack too, Brenna?" Beansprout asked.

"Yes," she answered from the darkness. "At the moment I live with Woodsmoke and his family. We're friends. I said I would travel to your world with him, for safety. And I was curious too. After meeting Jack, I wanted to know what your world was like."

"If Granddad's safe, then it must be all right here," Tom said.

"Your grandfather is with Fahey, in a safe area," Woodsmoke replied. "We are a long way from there."

While they were talking, faint sounds of strange music and singing started to fill the gorge. Then there was an almighty roaring sound and the clatter of what sounded like hooves racing along the path.

Woodsmoke jumped to his feet and peered from the entrance of the cave. "I think we've been found," he said over his shoulder.

Tom's heart beat faster, as if it would leap out of his chest. Beansprout waited motionless beside him. The rumbling and clattering became louder, accompanied by wild singing and laughing. A huge towering water spout erupted from the river, filling the cave with spray, before collapsing and leaving a murky green light to illuminate the night.

Woodsmoke stepped back as a large figure appeared in the cave entrance, a black shadow against the eerie green glow. A booming voice declared, "Welcome to the Eye, travellers." It didn't sound welcoming.

Woodsmoke replied with a bow, "Greetings, we thank you for your welcome."

The voice answered, "The Emperor is waiting to see you." He stepped aside, gesturing for them to leave.

As they made their way out of the cave, they saw below them dozens of horses, carrying men and women armed with swords and spears. The middle of the river was a boiling mass of giant tentacles, waving in the strange green light.

They scrambled down, and were each hustled on to a horse with another rider. The animals stamped impatiently until the four of them were seated, then wheeled round, heading back to the lake. Tom gripped his rider. He'd never been on a horse before and was convinced he was going to be thrown off.

The castle that had been beneath the water was now above it, hundreds of lights shining from the windows, bright against the black night. They rushed up the broad ramp, along the parapet, and swept onto the bridge that had previously crossed the lake, but which now led to huge gates and a courtyard beyond. The sheer black granite walls were slick with running water which cascaded down and through grates in the floor.

The riders shouted to each other as they dismounted. Tossing the reins to others who emerged from the shadows, they headed towards a broad entrance on the left of the courtyard.

Tom, Beansprout, Woodsmoke and Brenna stood uncertainly watching the movements around the courtyard, wondering where they were expected to go. Tom imagined deep dark dungeons, dank and cold. However, the man with the booming voice shepherded them into a large dining hall crowded with people eating and drinking at long tables. Servants milled around, replenishing enormous plates and dishes as the sound of music came from a group in the corner of the room.

Slowly, as everyone turned to look at them, the room fell silent.

A voice came from the far end of the room. "So, our visitors *finally* arrive in my hall."

Craning his neck, Tom saw a man, his dark hair streaked with grey, sitting at a table raised on a dais. He leaned forward on his ornate chair, looking at them intently. This must be the Emperor.

Woodsmoke and Brenna immediately bowed, a sweeping gesture reaching down to their feet, before Woodsmoke strode forward.

"I would like to apologise for our unannounced presence in the Eye," he said. "It was completely unplanned, and we were aiming to be out before disturbing Your Majesty."

"Were you indeed?" The Emperor's voice boomed out across the hall. "And what did you hope to achieve by visiting the Eye? Are you spies?"

"No! We are not spies. We came to rescue the human child who passed through the portal. It was an accident."

Tom felt all eyes fall on him and his cousin. He opened his mouth to take the blame, but before he could speak, Beansprout said in a shaky voice, "I'm sorry, Your Majesty. It was my fault. I didn't realise what would happen."

"So, human child, it is you that brings visitors to my hall." The Emperor peered closely at them both. "How did you find the doorway? It has surely been closed for many years."

"I saw a hole in the ground and found it that way."

"It was our fault," interrupted Woodsmoke. "We left the passage open. But I would like to reassure you that it is now closed, and with Your Majesty's permission we will leave tomorrow to return the visitors to their home. If you could direct us to a portal that would be most helpful."

"And what," said the Emperor, "are two of the fey from the Realm of Earth doing with humans? Didn't we stop passing to their world many hundreds of years ago?"

"I had to deliver a message. A guest came to our realm of late. He wanted to send a message to his family, telling them that he was safe."

The Emperor paused, his face stern as he stared at Woodsmoke. He spoke softly. "It has also been a very long time since anyone from the Realm of Earth came to the Eye."

Woodsmoke smiled a thin smile. "Too long. But you are not who we expected to see, Your Majesty."

After another long pause, during which there was only a breathless silence, the Emperor said, "No, I would not be. There have been many changes here." He gazed into the middle distance for a moment and then, suddenly relaxing, said, "Well, I would be a poor host if I did not offer you food. Come, sit, all of you, and you can tell me what is happening in your realm."

With that the general hum of noise started again. The people sitting around the Emperor moved aside to make room, and Tom and Beansprout sat on the Emperor's left, while Woodsmoke and Brenna sat to his right. The Emperor started talking to Woodsmoke and Brenna, leaving Tom and Beansprout to eat and think.

Servants put plates in front of them, and they helped themselves from platters in the centre of the table. There were whole baked fish the length of a man's arm; piles of mussels and oysters, and steaming bowls of fish stew. Tom took a bite of something green that was probably fried seaweed, and discretely spat the salty mouthful into a table napkin. Beansprout was merrily tucking into a huge bowl of trifle.

Looking around the room, Tom realised the other guests weren't really "people", in the usual sense of the word. Neither were Woodsmoke and Brenna. The Emperor had called them "fey".

Tom couldn't quite explain what made them different, other than a peculiar awareness they seemed to have. It was quite unnerving. When they looked at you, it was as if they could see right into your mind; could tell exactly what you were thinking. Even though he had no evidence of this, Tom felt he should try and hide his thoughts.

And Brenna could turn into a bird! He wondered if the people in the Eye could turn into animals too. They looked a little different to Woodsmoke and Brenna. Their skin was slightly shimmery, as if dusted with silver, and their eyes were a bright shiny blue. And the castle – what an amazing place! The hall was similar to the old English halls he'd seen in books, but instead of having fireplaces, there were fountains in alcoves along the wall. The water cooled the hall – a welcome change from the sticky heat outside.

Tom tried to look at the Emperor without being too obvious about it, watching him out of the corner of his eye. He was much younger than Tom had thought an Emperor would be. His hair was pulled up into a knot on his head, his face was sharp, his eyebrows high and quizzical, and he wore long loose robes of dark blue, which pooled like water at his feet. His chair looked as if it were made from polished coral.

Tom suddenly felt a long way from home. It was hard to believe that only this morning they were in the wood by his house. It was then that Tom realised his father would have no idea where he was, or Beansprout's mother, but there was nothing he could do now. He knew though that he still wanted to see his granddad before going back.

He was incredibly tired, and he noticed Beansprout's eyes beginning to close, her head nodding gently before she snapped it up, trying to stay awake. He turned to her. "You OK?"

"Exhausted, Tom. But I don't want to go to bed – there's too much to see. This is all so weird." She shook her head as she gazed around the room.

"Do you still want to find Granddad?" Tom asked.

"Yes. Absolutely! We're so close it would be mad not to. Woodsmoke will take us. We'll make him!"

"Good. Because I'm not ready to go home yet. This place was under water earlier, can you believe that? And nothing's wet. Well, not like you'd expect."

"Really? How does that happen? We have to stay. I don't want to go home yet, Tom."

The Emperor turned their way, saw Beansprout yawning, and immediately summoned a servant. "Give our guests a room each in the East Tower." Turning back to them he said, "You two are tired. You do not keep such late hours as we do. Sleep now and we will talk tomorrow."

It seemed they had little choice. Tom caught Woodsmoke's attention, and he nodded, so they followed the servant out of the hall.

He led them along winding corridors and up stairs grand and sweeping and small and spiralling, until they were completely disorientated. They ended up on a short corridor and were shown rooms next to each other. Tom lay on his bed thinking he'd be awake all night, but in minutes he was fast asleep.

5 The Cavern of the Four Portals

Several hours later, Tom woke feeling groggy and disorientated, and for a few seconds couldn't work out where he was. He struggled to open his eyes – his eyelids felt as heavy as lead.

Events from the previous day began to filter into his thoughts, and he sat up in bed, looking wildly around the room. Then he remembered – he was in the bedroom in the tower. Flopping back down, he wondered if this was what jetlag felt like.

His dreams started to return to him. Again the white-haired woman had appeared, but this time the image had been sharper, clearer. She'd looked impatient, saying, "Come, Tom, you are nearly here. Hurry! There are things you must do." Again firelight had filled his vision and he'd felt its heat; chanting had filled his ears.

With a shock he realised it had been her voice in his head when they'd crossed the portal. Who was she? What things must he do?

He brushed off the dream and looked round the room, which was filled with a dull green light. Why was the room green? Were there leaves over the window? Then he had another thought. Were they back under the water? He jumped out of bed and ran to the window. That was definitely water.

The lake floor was of smooth rock and sand. Large tree-like plants waved about in the current, their thick knotted roots anchored into the rock. Fish of all sizes swam past the window, and horses grazed on the lake floor. Looking up, he saw a pale yellow disc, and the surface of the lake glinting like a mirror far above. Shafts of sunlight pierced the gloom.

The urge to explore woke him fully. On a table in the corner of his room was a bowl of steaming water, a bar of soap, and towels. He had a quick wash and raked his fingers through his hair. Wondering if Beansprout was awake he stepped into the empty corridor and knocked on her door. "Come in," he heard her call.

She was at the window, staring into the water. "Tom! You're right, we're under the water. How is this possible?"

"Magic, I guess."

"But how do we get out of here? We're trapped."

"I'm more worried about how we find breakfast! Fancy a wander?"

"Should we? What if we get lost?"

"Oh we'll definitely get lost, but we're lost anyway, aren't we?" He shrugged and smiled.

Grabbing their packs, they headed down the corridor, attempting to retrace their steps from the night before. They met no one, and the castle was eerily silent. Before long it was clear they were lost – these ornate hallways were different to those they had walked along the night before. The walls were hung with tapestries of underwater scenes, and decorated with the skeletal remains of unfamiliar creatures. Rills of water trickled down the edges of the corridors, and there were small pools filled with lily pads, and plants that they didn't recognise.

"I think we're in the main part of the castle, Tom," Beansprout whispered. They had come to a large circular space with a grand staircase leading down to an atrium. Huge windows let in the green glow of the water, and large purple fronds of aquatic plants tapped against the panes.

As they reached the atrium, a door opened and a woman stepped out. She looked surprised for the briefest of seconds, and then smiled. "You must be our human visitors. Follow me."

On the far side of the atrium, a wooden arched doorway led to a courtyard. Above them, water was suspended from its downward rush by some mysterious force.

"Don't worry," the Emperor called. "It's quite safe." He was seated at a stone table laden with food and what looked like a pot of tea. "Come and join me, I have lots to ask you."

They sat while he poured tea – which was most definitely not normal tea – and offered them fish for breakfast. Tom took a sip of the green liquid; it was an odd-tasting salty brew.

"Woodsmoke has been telling me how you came to be here. I trust you are enjoying yourselves?"

Tom answered, trying to swallow his food quickly. "Yes. It's … different."

"Years ago," said the Emperor, thoughtfully, "many people from your world visited here – accidentally, of course – but it was easier then. The doorways were simpler to find and the walls between our worlds came and went. Only those who know where to look visit now, and few have this knowledge. Those who do come are not always friendly." He looked regretful.

"It has also been a long time since we saw anyone from the Realm of Earth," he continued. "As I explained to your friends last night, I have been Emperor since my father died, and things have been difficult." Tom and Beansprout carried on eating and nodding. "My father was suspicious and treated visitors badly – I understand why your friends were worried about being here. He would probably have fed you to the Mantis."

Beansprout's face grew pale.

"We have tried to keep my father's death a secret. This has allowed me to make changes and defeat certain groups, particularly the swamp goblins."

Noticing Beansprout's discomfort, he changed the subject. "Tell me all about you. I once visited your world, when the forests ran thick, tangled and unbroken right to the shores of your seas. What is it like now?"

Between them they attempted to answer his question, and were on to their third pot of "tea", when Woodsmoke and Brenna appeared, looking more relaxed than the day before, and not in the slightest concerned at the water suspended high above their heads.

"Last night," the Emperor nodded at Woodsmoke, "I agreed to escort you to our closest portal to the Realm of Earth. Unfortunately my father destroyed many portals, particularly those to your world," he said, looking at Tom and Beansprout, "so I cannot send you home. But I think you are not displeased with that?" He looked amused at their excited faces.

"We still want to find our grandfather," said Tom, glaring at Woodsmoke, who rolled his eyes.

"Yes, yes. All right," said Woodsmoke. "We'll see

where we end up. But I'm not promising anything!"

"Obviously my father didn't succeed in completely destroying the portals," said the Emperor, "otherwise you wouldn't be here. But I would instead suggest that we escort you up the river that runs to the border. It will be a difficult journey, passing through swamps and then the mangrove forests, which, at this time of year, are full of flesh flies, and it could take many weeks–"

"No," said Woodsmoke. "It would take far too long. We have to attempt the portal."

"Very well then. We shall leave tonight."

After the sun had set, and the water around them had become black and impenetrable, the castle rose majestically to the surface of the lake. It was a discomforting experience to find themselves shooting upwards, the floor rocking beneath them as if there was an earthquake. The roar of water filled the castle and Tom felt his ears become thick with pressure, all sound becoming muffled, before they popped and everything returned to normal.

The castle doors were thrown open and fresh air began to circulate, getting rid of the stuffiness that had built up during the day.

Accompanied by the Emperor and a dozen men carrying lanterns, they exited the castle through the rear gate. Passing over the stone bridge, they paused at the rocky ledge.

"We'll just summon the hippocamps," said the Emperor.

"Sea horses," said Woodsmoke, in response to Tom's baffled expression.

One of the Emperor's men pulled a flute out of his pocket and blew into it.

"I can't hear anything," Beansprout said.

"I expect it's too high-pitched for our ears," Tom answered.

Moments later, four horses broke the surface, whinnying softly as they swam towards the shore. They had normal horse heads, but the manes trailing down their backs were webbed and transparent. Small wings sprouted from their sides, and large fishtails propelled them through the water.

"They're so beautiful," Beansprout said, leaning forward to pat them.

"Oh yes, and quite tame," the Emperor said. He turned and led the way to one side of the waterfall, pushing through lush ferns into a partially hidden cleft in the rock. Tom followed the Emperor down a passageway that opened into a wider tunnel, through which rushed a fast-flowing river. In one direction the river emptied into the lake; in the other it ran along the tunnel into darkness.

The hippocamps were waiting for them beside a small ship. There were no sails; instead Tom saw neatly stacked oars alongside rows of seats.

The men harnessed the animals to the front before boarding the vessel, hanging their lanterns along the sides and on the prow. Tom, Beansprout, Woodsmoke and Brenna made their way to the stern with the Emperor. When everyone was seated, they gently pushed out.

The air in the tunnel was damp and the walls trickled with water. Beyond the ship the darkness was absolute. Their progress was slow but steady.

The Emperor turned to them. "We have had much rain lately so the river should be deep enough to take us all the way to the portal. In places the current is swift and strong, so don't fall in."

"How far does the river go?" asked Tom.

"Oh, miles and miles – far beyond our destination. But it becomes narrower, and then you have to climb. There are many waterfalls, and places where the water completely fills the caverns. The traveller must take great care to avoid those. And the river often branches in two. It is easy to become lost. People have entered here and never been seen again." He paused, then added, "You're lucky the portal didn't bring you here when you arrived." His words hung in the air and seemed to echo in the enclosed space.

Tom felt a cold shudder run down his spine as he realised they could have emerged anywhere. "Could we have ended up in the sea?"

"Oh yes, the portals can be quite hazardous."

Understatement of the year. Tom turned to Woodsmoke and Brenna. "Could we come out somewhere really bad in your realm?"

Brenna nodded. "Yes, but we know our world well, so hopefully we will be fine. We may still have further to travel than we would want, though."

Woodsmoke added a word of warning. "This place is not for the unprepared traveller, Tom. Like your own world, ours has areas that are hostile to outsiders."

"Blimey," said Beansprout, "I wish I'd known that before I stuck my hand in."

"This reminds me of the Greek ships I've seen in history books," said Tom.

"Ah, how clever of you Tom! It is in fact a version of the trireme, one of the ships we introduced to the Greeks. We were very influential in the Mediterranean many years ago. We are a seafaring people–"

"Really?" interrupted Tom, disbelief in his voice. "You helped the Greeks?"

"Oh, only slightly," the Emperor answered, modestly. "Not me personally – I was far too young. Unfortunately we are also responsible for the presence of the giant squid and sea serpents in your seas. An accidental crossing from our world."

Tom now had so many questions whizzing around his head, he didn't know which to ask first. "Sea serpents? But they're a myth. And how old are you? That was over two thousand years ago!"

The Emperor looked at the floor and scratched his chin. "Well, I am older than I look. We are a race that lives for many years. Woodsmoke and Brenna are much older than you imagine."

Beansprout, who had been following the conversation with some interest, butted in. "So how old *are* you two?"

Woodsmoke laughed. "I am four hundred and twenty-three years old – quite young, really. What about you, Brenna?"

"Oh, three hundred and seventy, or thereabouts," she said with a wry smile.

"If you're interested in sea creatures, Tom," the Emperor said, "we may see one later. Or perhaps you're not *that* interested," he added, noting Tom's expression.

"Where might we see one?" Tom asked nervously.

"We are going to the Cavern of the Four Portals – although there are of course only three now. It's a huge cave, and the river there forms a deep lake connected by a passageway to the sea. One of our greatest explorers found it. Unfortunately, on occasions a giant dectopus swims up the passageway and takes up residence in the lake. If it's there, we must try not to disturb it." He looked at their worried faces and added, "I'm sure we won't."

"What's a dectopus?" Tom asked.

"It is a ten-tentacled sea creature. Haven't you heard of them?"

"I've only heard of an octopus."

"Well, there you are then. Much the same, just a bit bigger."

For a while they fell silent, listening to the sound of the hippocamps splashing in the inky black river. At least, Tom hoped it was the hippocamps ...

A while later the river started to curl to the left and the passageway became bigger. The walls were slick with moisture, the torchlight slipping off the walls and up to the roof or down to the water, where it was swallowed by the unrelenting blackness.

"Water is leaking through the rock," the Emperor said. "This section of the tunnel is quite porous." Stalactites hung from the roof, and streaks of pink and yellow glimmered like underground rainbows.

It seemed as if they had been in the tunnel for hours, and Tom became more and more aware of the huge amount of rock over their heads as they moved still further underground. Tributaries opened up on either side, and water poured down from the suffocating blackness. Tom peered up the tunnels, seeing nothing, but hearing strange gurgles and splashes. Every now and again the Emperor would impart some bit of knowledge about the warren of tunnels and mysterious whirlpools they were passing, but their worried faces eventually drove him to silence.

Just as Tom was beginning to think the journey would never end, the passage opened up, and the light from the ship was swallowed up by the bigger space. The Emperor touched the wick from his lantern to the wall, and a band of bright orange flame raced along the rock face. He did the same on the other side of the passage, and the cavern became brighter as the flames spread in a circle beneath a domed roof. Craning his neck, Tom saw huge, elaborate carvings on the walls towering above him, depicting fights between enormous sea creatures. They seemed to move in the flickering light.

They headed to a pier jutting out into the far side of the lake, beyond which was a broad stone floor on which boxes and ropes were coiled. Behind the boxes, steps led to a dark shadowy recess like the one through which Tom and Beansprout had passed. They had reached the portals.

He turned to the Emperor. "What are all the boxes for?"

"This is where we built the ship. And we store other things here, for journeying further inland." He nodded to the rear of the cavern where the river exited into another tunnel.

As they passed the centre of the pool, bubbles appeared on the surface. The hippocamps became nervous, snorting wildly and straining towards the shore. Seeing the commotion, the men raised their short sharp tridents, and stood peering into the water.

"Is it the dectopus?" said Beansprout.

No one answered. Woodsmoke raised his longbow, keeping his eyes on the water, and Brenna pulled her sword free from its scabbard.

The Emperor touched Tom and Beansprout gently on the arm, pulling them back from the side of the ship. "Stay in the middle."

The hippocamps pulled furiously towards the shore.

Then, in front of them, a sleek and scaly tentacle uncoiled on the surface before plunging into the depths again. For a few seconds the water fell still, then several more tentacles appeared, followed by the enormous bulbous body of the dectopus. It reared into the air, water streaming over it. Its skin was wrinkled and thick like elephant's, and two enormous eyes blinked slowly. It flicked several tentacles towards them, and Tom saw its suckers raised and ready to grasp the ship.

Beansprout screamed; Woodsmoke released several arrows at its head. Some found their target, but most bounced off into the water. Before Woodsmoke could fire again, the dectopus plunged back beneath the surface, making the boat rock wildly.

"He wasn't kidding when he said giant dectopus!" Tom exclaimed.

The hippocamps raced forward, but the dectopus rose again, this time on the starboard side of the ship. Shadows from the flames writhed across its mottled deep-purple skin. Another volley of arrows left Woodsmoke's bow, but again the dectopus's tentacles whipped across the surface of the pool. One grabbed a hippocamp, lifting it as if it were a toy, ripping it free of its harness and dropping it into its gaping mouth. Other tentacles latched onto the ship, causing it to lurch wildly. Everyone grabbed for something fixed; Tom slid across the deck and hit the side, hurting his elbow. Brenna rolled and quickly regained her feet, slashing at the closest tentacle. The dectopus roared in pain, the noise echoing around the cave, but the ship tipped further. Woodsmoke and the Emperor joined Brenna, and the three slashed at the tentacles as the men released a volley of tridents. With another roar the tentacles finally released the ship, which shot upright, waves rolling across the deck.

The remaining hippocamps had broken free and were racing away with deafening shrieks that echoed around the cave. Then they disappeared beneath the surface of the water.

"Start rowing!" the Emperor yelled. They were within reach of the pier when the dectopus rose again, directly ahead. It towered above them, and this time its tentacles grabbed both sides of the boat, pulling it towards its open mouth. A tentacle whipped across their heads, its huge suckers flexing like white mouths. It grabbed one of the Emperor's men. With a scream he was dropped into its waiting mouth.

"Abandon ship!" commanded the Emperor, as they were dragged ever closer to the dectopus's waiting mouth.

Tom grabbed Beansprout and pushed her forward. "Go!" he shouted. "I'll follow."

Beansprout leapt into the mass of frothing churning water. Tom followed, gasping as he hit the icy lake. It was so cold it felt like a fist was squeezing his lungs. The water blinded and deafened him, and he flailed around, desperately trying to reach the surface, his clothes heavy and billowing around him. His head emerged and he gasped for air.

He was surrounded by seething water and thrashing tentacles. Did it only have ten tentacles? It seemed like so many more. He heard an enormous splintering crash, and watched as a chunk of the boat was ripped off and sent flying overhead.

As he started swimming for the shore, a hippocamp appeared beneath him and he grasped its webbed mane. It raced through the water, tipping him off in the shallows. Once clear of the water he turned, then quickly ducked and rolled as a tentacle whipped towards him. It slapped the ground, it suckers slurping.

He saw Beansprout lying exhausted nearby and dragged himself to her side. "Run!" he yelled, grabbing her arm. Together they raced for the back of the cave, their wet clothes flapping around them.

Woodsmoke and Brenna had also managed to jump free of the boat and were pulled swiftly to shore by the hippocamps. The water was still a churning mass of men and tentacles. Some made it to the shore, while others disappeared beneath the surface.

Woodsmoke took up position at the shattered end of the pier, firing a blur of arrows. Brenna began helping the men who'd made it out of the water gather a pile of silvery-looking ropes. At the bow of his shattered ship, the Emperor looked towards the shore before diving into the water.

The dectopus pursued those still in the lake. Although the men were fast, some weren't fast enough. Those who made it to the shore climbed up to where several large pieces of machinery hung high on the rock walls. Thick silvery ropes ran from these to a giant web suspended over the pool.

The Emperor emerged in the middle of the churning lake before dipping out of sight again. The dectopus darted towards him. For several seconds nothing happened, and the water became smooth and still. Just as Tom began to worry that the Emperor had drowned, he surfaced right under the web and shouted, "Now!"

The dectopus rose above the surface as the Emperor disappeared, and before it could follow him, the giant web dropped, along with several hundredweight of stone it had supported. An enormous boom rang out as the weight crashed down onto the creature, which sank below the surface. A large wave rose and raced to the shore and with it came the Emperor, who landed on the rocky edge.

"Quickly," he shouted. "Secure him with the ropes!" His remaining men dived back into the water, dragging the ropes behind them. This time they were submerged for a long time.

"How can they stay under water for so long?" asked Beansprout.

Woodsmoke answered, joining them from the pier. "They're water spirits. That's why their skin is silvery looking, almost as if they are half fish. They can swim under water for hours. They just don't live in it."

"And what was the web thing under the roof?"

"Giant water spiders make very strong webs!"

Beansprout looked a little sick. "I hope we don't meet one of those too."

6 In the Greenwood

While the Emperor and his men finished their tasks under water, Woodsmoke lit a fire from the woodpile he found in a dry corner and they warmed themselves by the bright flames. They were still shocked by their violent encounter.

"That was too close for comfort," Woodsmoke said.

"Too close for some of the men," Brenna said sadly.

"And the hippocamp," Beansprout added.

"I take it you've seen the portals?" Woodsmoke gestured to the shadowy recess above them.

Tom nodded. "I suppose we'll leave when the Emperor gets back?"

"Yes. We're lucky he was feeling generous. We would never have found this place without him."

"Who built the portals?"

"They were built thousands of years ago, by the powerful magic of the ancient gods."

"Oh." That wasn't the answer Tom had expected. "What gods?"

"That tale's for another time, Tom," Woodsmoke said.

"And will you take us to our grandfather? Please, Woodsmoke. We're so close."

"I suppose so. And anyway, I don't know of any other portal to take you to your world, apart from the one we used. We don't have a choice."

Beansprout gave Woodsmoke a beaming smile.

The Emperor and his men finally emerged from the deep cold waters and shook the water off their skin like otters.

"All done," said the Emperor with a faint smile. "We have wrapped it up so tightly it will take weeks to break free, if it ever does. And now I'm starved. Fish, anyone?"

His men brought a dozen large rainbow-scaled fish from the half-ruined boat, lit a second fire and spread the fish on flat grills to cook. Water and wine were handed out, and they sat talking while the smell of cooking fish filled the air.

"I'm sorry you've lost men," said Woodsmoke. "I feel it's our fault. It wouldn't have happened if you hadn't brought us here. We owe you a huge debt."

"Not at all. It's happened before and will no doubt happen again. We risk these encounters all the time when we travel, and although it's sad to lose men, we accept it. I'm tempted to pass through the portal with you, but the realm remains unsettled and I still have much to do here. Another time."

He paused to rummage in his pockets, and pulled out a curious spiral shell inlaid with silver and jade. Muttering a few words, he passed his hand across it.

"A present," he said, "to remember your time in the Eye. Any time you need help and there's water nearby, just throw it in. I won't tell you what will happen. It will be a surprise. Which of you would like to look after it?"

"Thank you. Tom should," Beansprout said immediately.

"Thanks," said Tom, hoping he wouldn't lose it as he slipped it into his pocket.

After eating, they gathered their things and walked up the stone steps to the portals high above the lake. Carvings of beasts marched beside the path, as if accompanying them.

They stood before the three doorways. At the far end was a mass of rubble where once a fourth had stood. Tom wouldn't have thought it possible to destroy these doorways; they looked as if they would stand forever.

The portal to the Realm of Earth was in the middle, surrounded by carvings of trees, mountains, and strange hoof-footed half-men. Directly over the arch were carvings of a woman with a serene face, and a man with enormous antlers rising from his head.

"Time to go," said Woodsmoke. Holding hands, they stepped through the archway and passed out of the Realm of Water.

With a rush and a swooping, falling motion, Tom felt the blackness slide by and heard fluttering, just for a moment, until they landed with a thump. This time he felt soft earth, a loamy richness beneath his hands.

It was quiet, the eerie silence before dawn, with the barest suggestion of light. There was a faint pulsing of wind, as if something was breathing, and the air was crisp and sharp, carrying the smell of snow and pine.

They waited in silence for the light to grow, and as it did, birds started to sing. Before long the air was thick with birdsong, long looping notes smothering the silence. The sunrise revealed a pine forest, the trunks pressed close, the branches knotted together just above their heads. A thick mist silvered the ground.

"We're on the mountain," Brenna murmured, "on the lower slopes. Can you smell the snow?"

Woodsmoke nodded. "Come."

The ground sloped away in front of them, and despite the rising sun, the light remained dim. The birds fell silent. Beneath their feet, the thick carpet of pine needles swallowed their footsteps. Mist swirled around their legs in whispery tendrils, rising almost unnoticed, until the others had disappeared from Tom's view. Distracted by his new surroundings, he wandered down a tunnel that hollowed out in the mist before him. Passing through it, he found himself in a clearing. The sweet pungent scent of honeysuckle perfumed the air.

There was no sign of the others. A woman sat cross-legged in the centre of the clearing. She was beautiful, with long white hair framing her pale face. She seemed both very young and very old. Her eyes were pale green, and she wore a long grey dress trimmed with fur. With a shock, Tom realised she was the woman he had seen in his dreams.

She gazed at him, and without seeming to speak, said, "Tom, at last you have arrived. Come and sit so we can talk."

Trapped within the circle of mist, he warily moved closer.

She smiled. "So, Tom, I have called you here because there is something you must do."

"I think you're confusing me with someone else," he said crossly. "I came here to find my grandfather and take him home. Who are you? How do you know my name, and how did you get into my dreams?"

"But Tom," she said, ignoring his questions. "What if he doesn't want to return home?"

"Of course he will, why wouldn't he?" Tom felt a slight panic as he answered; a sense of unease as other possibilities suggested themselves.

Ignoring his question again, she said, "There is something else I want you to do while you are here."

"What could you possibly want me to do?" he asked, increasingly confused by the conversation.

"I need you to wake the King who lies sleeping on the Isle of Avalon. Your grandfather's friend Fahey once tried to wake the King, many years ago, but it wasn't time and I sent him far from here. However, Queen Gavina has become dangerous; she hunts her own people, the Aerikeen. This is the time to wake the King, and you are the one who must wake him."

Tom sat there dumbfounded. "What king? On where? How can I wake him if this Fahey, or whatever his name is, couldn't?"

"Because you have something Fahey didn't."

The woman held out a supple, fresh, living twig, ripe with spring growth.

"This will enable you to wake the King. Only with the bough can you do this."

Tom felt panic building in him again. "But how? I don't know where this place is. What king? Why me? And who are you?"

"Ask Woodsmoke. He can show you the way. It is important Tom. The Queen's people need your help. You are linked to the King by your blood, and only someone of his blood can wake him. And you must hurry. You have taken far too long to get here." There was a hint of impatience in her tone.

Too long? What was she talking about? Just as he was about to ask, Tom felt a weight in his lap and, looking down, saw that the twig had magically appeared there, and had turned from a living branch to solid silver. He picked it up, wondering how she had managed such a clever trick.

As he held it, a ball of light grew within the woman until it was so bright that Tom had to close his eyes and cover them with his hands. When the light faded, she had gone, and he was sitting alone in bright sunshine.

Tom sat dazed. The distant shouts of his friends finally disturbed his trance, and he stumbled to his feet. "I'm here, over here!" he called.

A large, black, glossy-plumed bird burst into the clearing and, spotting him, swooped off again. Brenna, gone to guide the others.

When they finally found him, Beansprout was exasperated. "Tom, where have you been? We've been calling for hours!"

Brenna turned to Woodsmoke. "I swear I flew over here earlier, but I couldn't see him!"

Woodsmoke said, "Are you OK, Tom? You look odd."

"I've had a weird encounter."

"What do you mean? With whom?"

"A really old woman with long white hair, dressed in grey. Except she didn't seem old. Not really."

Brenna and Woodsmoke stood gaping at Tom. Brenna gathered herself first. "You met the Lady of the Lake?"

"I don't know. Did I?" Tom shrugged.

"What did she want, Tom?"

"She said I have to wake the King."

Woodsmoke groaned and sat suddenly on the ground, as if his legs had given way. Brenna patted his shoulder in sympathy and sat next to him. For a while they sat silently, deep in thought, while Tom wondered where he'd heard the woman's name before.

Beansprout broke the silence. "Will someone please tell me what's going on? Who's the King that Tom has to wake? Why is he asleep?"

"Years ago," Woodsmoke said, "there was a famous king. He was much loved, and saved the ancient Britons from attack many times. He was given a magical sword, and he had the help of a powerful wizard. Does this ring any bells for you?"

"It sounds like King Arthur," Tom said.

"That's exactly who it is. He has been asleep for centuries, and now it seems you must wake him."

Tom stared at Woodsmoke. "But he died. At least fifteen hundred years ago – if he ever existed at all."

"Oh, he was real, Tom. It is said he will reappear when he's most needed. Our stories say he will awaken here."

"But he's dead."

Woodsmoke shook his head. "No, he's asleep – a deep enchanted sleep, in a tomb on the Isle of Avalon. In exchange for the sword, Excalibur, Merlin made a deal with the fey, and therefore so did Arthur, and close to death he was brought here to rest until he was needed again. The island can only be reached by summoning the Lady of the Lake who will take you across on a boat. It's old magic, Tom."

"How do you know all this?"

"Because my grandfather is a bard, a teller of stories, and that was his favourite. Arthur was the king my grandfather tried to wake."

"The woman told me that, but she said it was the wrong time and he was the wrong person. So why did he try to wake him?"

"He was curious and it seemed like fun."

Tom looked at him suspiciously. "Really?"

"You'll see when you meet him." He rolled his eyes. "But I don't understand why we need the King now."

"She said something about Queen Gavina 'hunting her own.' What does that mean?"

Woodsmoke looked with alarm at Brenna. She went pale and stuttered, "I suppose that means she's hunting her own people. But why would she do that?" She stared at Tom. "How are you to wake him? She must have said."

"She told me to use this." Tom produced the silver twig with a flourish. "And she said you would show me the way, Woodsmoke. And that we should hurry."

"Did she now?" Woodsmoke took the silver twig off him, examining it closely. "I have no idea what this is, but Fahey might. We need to get back home as soon as possible. Come on, let's go." And with that he stood up and gestured down through the forest and to the west. "We know where we are, and that's where we need to go."

Tom stood, putting the silver twig in his pack. He extended a hand to Beansprout, pulling her to her feet.

"I don't understand," she said, frowning. "Why do you have to do this?"

Tom laughed. "Something about me being his blood."

"What?" she exclaimed. "So you're related to King Arthur?"

"Mmm, I suppose so."

"So I am too?"

"I don't know. She didn't say. Maybe it's on my mum's side?"

With a shrug he strolled off after the others, leaving

Beansprout open-mouthed behind him.

The pines thinned out, and became mixed with oak, birch and beech trees. Spring flowers grew underfoot, and the scent of blossom filled the air. The powerful feeling of magic had gone, but Tom could still feel a tingle, like static. Woodsmoke strode ahead, while Brenna flew most of the time.

Woodsmoke explained that when they left the wood, they would enter the orchard terraces that ran above the river, adding that he'd heard rumours about attacks from the wood sprites that had left Aeriken Forest to hunt further afield.

Tom laughed. "What? Tiny little wood sprites with bells on their hats? How can they be dangerous?"

"Because they are not small," said Brenna, "and they have vicious sharp teeth. In fact, they are deadly hunters."

"Oh," was all Tom could think of to reply.

Beansprout smirked. "Idiot."

They had been walking for hours and the sun was sinking into the west. The woodland was now behind them, on the slopes of the mountain. The pines straggled upwards to meet the snow, which glowed in the fading light. The peak was lost in clouds. Beyond the mountain was a series of ridges retreating into a misty blueness.

They snaked down the slopes and across broad sprawling terraces, filled with unruly trees covered in blossom. Mouldy fruit was rotting on the ground. Between the trees the grass grew tall, and they stumbled over fallen branches and abandoned tools.

"What happened here?" Beansprout asked.

"The wood sprites have been busy," said Woodsmoke. "Everyone's abandoned this place. Be careful –

we don't know if the sprites are still close."

They progressed steadily through the deserted terraces. About halfway down they heard the river roaring in the distance, and saw a collection of stone buildings which looked abandoned.

"Perfect," said Woodsmoke, "we can stay here for the night."

Cautiously he entered the closest one. Inside, baskets were strewn across the floor, and wooden tables had been overturned, suggesting a fight.

In the corner was a ladder leading to the upper floor. Brenna pulled her sword free and climbed up, peering slowly over the edge. "It's empty," she called down.

Woodsmoke looked at Tom. "Come with me, we'll check the other buildings." Tom was glad to help. He'd felt useless in the cavern when the dectopus attacked, and now he'd been told he had to wake the King he felt he should prove his worth. As they entered the other buildings he stood watch at the door while Woodsmoke checked inside.

Once satisfied there was no one else there, they strolled to the far edge of the terraces and Woodsmoke pulled out his longbow, saying, "I'll see if I can get us some dinner."

Tom watched him for a few moments and then asked, "Is waking the King dangerous?"

Woodsmoke kept his gaze ahead. "I have no idea, Tom. I'm sure it won't be easy."

"But you will help me get there?"

"Of course. We'll take you to the lakeshore, but I don't know what to expect any more than you do. I wonder what the Queen is up to?" He quickly released three arrows, which disappeared in the long grass. "Dinner," he said, strolling over to pick up the limp rabbits.

7 Beneath the Hill

The evening was uneventful. They were all tired and hungry, and thankful for Woodsmoke's rabbit stew. After collecting sacking from the floor to use as blankets, they were soon asleep.

The next morning the four carried on towards the river, a ribbon of light in the distance. Tom was distracted by thoughts of the silver twig and waking the King. He didn't know how he was going to do it, but couldn't help feeling excited. He had read so many stories about King Arthur and his knights; he tried to imagine what he would be like. Occasionally he glanced back to where Beansprout lagged behind, stopping often to gaze across the landscape. Exasperated, he shouted, "Beansprout, keep up!"

She ignored him, giving an occasional wave to keep him happy, and eventually he gave up, figuring she'd catch up when they stopped.

The sun burned hot and the day was still, without a breath of wind. Tom was also distracted, by strange sounds around him. Every now and then he heard singing, and sometimes whispering, but he couldn't work out where the sound was coming from. It was always just out of reach, and when he thought it was getting louder, it disappeared completely.

At last they reached the river, which meandered across the base of the terraces, separating them from the broad flower-filled meadows beyond. Out of the meadows rose a large mound that glowed a fierce green, vigorous with life, drawing their gaze.

The river was too wide and deep to cross, so they headed for a stone bridge they could see in the distance. It was a high, single-spanned arch, and as they got closer they saw that big chunks of stone had fallen, tumbling into the river below. Woodsmoke went across first, saying, "Tread carefully, and let's keep some distance between us."

Brenna flew ahead while Woodsmoke kept to the edge by the low stone wall, avoiding gaping holes beneath which the water passed lazily.

The large mound, a perfect half-sphere and covered with smooth cropped grass, was now over to their left. They followed the road from the bridge, and as they drew level with the mound they heard a deep rumbling sound, which travelled up through Tom's feet and into his chest. He stopped and looked around with alarm. A large dark opening appeared in the side of the hill, and out of it came bloodcurdling cries. A crowd of what Tom assumed to be wood sprites came pouring from the open doorway, heading across the meadows towards them. They were tall, their limbs sinewy with muscle, and there was a faint greenish tinge to their skin.

Woodsmoke yelled, "Wood sprites! Tom, Beansprout, get behind me!" Ahead of them, Brenna swooped down to earth, turned back into her humanlike form and pulled her sword from its scabbard.

Turning, Tom saw that Beansprout was still some way behind them. He couldn't tell if she'd seen what was happening, but hoped she would stay where she was – it would be safer.

Woodsmoke and Tom raced across the meadows to Brenna's side. She relentlessly attacked the sprites, ploughing through the middle of them, her sword flashing in the sunlight. Some of the sprites fell at her feet, covered in blood. Arrows from Woodsmoke's bow hissed through the air, thudding into the sprites. They stumbled and fell and were trampled by others close behind them.

As Tom grew closer he could see their lips pulled back as they whooped, their sharp teeth gleaming, but it seemed they were only after Brenna. She ran backwards, towards Tom and Woodsmoke, but there were too many sprites. A large net was thrown over her, knocking her to the ground, and she disappeared from view.

Tom and Woodsmoke were trapped. Some of the sprites had separated from the pack and blocked them from Brenna. Tom rolled to the ground, trying to fight his way through legs and spears, but the butts jammed repeatedly into him. He frantically scrabbled around and finally fought his way clear, staggering to his feet, bloodied and bruised, only to see the main pack dragging Brenna behind them through the dark doorway. He raced towards them and then, hearing thundering footsteps behind him, dived into the long grass. In seconds the last few sprites passed him, and he heard the groan of the doorway starting to close. With one final effort, Tom threw himself into the narrowing entrance before it clanged shut behind him.

He lay breathless, his face against the floor, for precious seconds, hoping he would go undetected. As the sprites' shouts faded down a corridor to his left, he sat up, his back pressed against the doorway.

If he had given any thought to what was inside the mound, he would have imagined a warren of corridors made from earth and rock. But it was far from that. He was in an ornate, richly carved passageway stretching to his left and right. The roof was high overhead, arched and glinting with a silver inlay, while the floor beneath him was shiny black marble. Directly ahead was a broad set of stairs climbing steeply upwards into blackness.

The sprites had headed left, so that was the way he must go. He took a few deep breaths to steady himself and started creeping down the passageway. Before long the light became brighter and he heard voices and laughter. Peering cautiously around a bend, he saw a small group of wood sprites talking, and no way of going around them. He'd have to turn back and find Brenna another way. She should be safe for now; he had the feeling that if they'd wanted to kill her, she'd be dead already. He decided to try to understand the layout of the mound so that when he found her, he'd know how to get out.

He retraced his steps and then followed the path to the right. It ran in a gentle curve, following the contours of the hill. Veins of gold and silver illuminated the walls and floors with a dim light, and clusters of glowing jewel-like stones hung like tempting fruit from the high ceiling. Steps ran off the path to lower levels, but he ignored them, and soon came to an antechamber lit by three torches that flamed and flickered on the walls. He cautiously opened one of the three doors leading off the chamber. The room beyond glowed with the same faint light. There was no one in sight.

The room was magnificent. There were shelves full of books, and more were stacked on the floor, on desks and on chairs. He ran his hands along their covers and wondered what the strange curled writing meant. On the walls were carved wood panels and large, richly embroidered tapestries. But the room had no other doorways – it was a dead end.

The second room was equally magnificent. It was like a reception room, with sofas and well-padded chairs. The third door led to another corridor, but this became so winding and twisted, and there were so many turnings off it, that Tom became afraid he would get lost, so he carefully retraced his steps.

Back in the antechamber he followed the original corridor back to the entrance, and then climbed up the staircase. There was no sign of the wood sprites, and Tom was so intrigued at what appeared to be a palace under the hill that he forgot to be afraid. At the top of the stairs was another antechamber and an ornate double doorway. Passing through it he found himself in a huge mirrored ballroom barely lit by the pale silvery light. He pulled a torch out of his backpack and shone the beam around the room, angling it quickly downwards when shattered light sparkled at him from all directions.

Piles of clothing were strewn across the ballroom floor. He picked his way through, and then, stooping to take a closer look, nearly dropped his torch in shock. He leapt backwards, his heart pounding.

These weren't just clothes. There were people inside them.

At first Tom thought they were dead, but as he looked closer he realised they were sleeping. Hundreds of them – not people, he saw, but faeries, with high arched eyebrows and a slight point to their ears, lying where they must have fallen, in a deep enchanted sleep.

Dust lay across their clothes and faces, and flew up from the floor as he walked. He tried not to sneeze. This was the creepiest thing he'd ever seen. With every step he took, he thought one of them would awake and grab his foot, but he kept moving. He could see doorways leading off to other rooms, also filled with enchanted faeries. They had fallen asleep upon chairs and tables, their faces landing on plates of food, their drinks abandoned.

His ears were playing tricks on him – he thought he heard whispers as soft, violet-scented breezes caressed his face. He repeated to himself, "They're asleep, they're asleep, keep going."

He crossed to doors on the far side of the room and found they opened onto a long broad balcony with stairs at either end. The balcony was also filled with sleepers, and it was here that Tom nearly gave himself away.

Below him was a vast hall, dominated by a cavernous fireplace in which blazed a huge fire. And there were more sleeping faeries. And wood sprites – dozens of them. Quickly turning off his torch, Tom dropped down next to the sleepers and wriggled forward to peer through the carved railings.

They seemed to be celebrating, probably because they'd captured Brenna. They passed round drinks, shouting and singing, while a smaller group clustered together, their heads close, their voices hushed. Tom could smell roasting meat, and his stomach rumbled.

One of the wood sprites stood and banged on a long table that ran the length of the room. When he had the others' attention he shouted, "At last we have someone to offer the Queen. We will leave at dark to meet the others and take her subject to her, then we will be assured of her help!"

At this there was a roar of pleasure from the crowd.

"Are you pleased, Duke?" He looked to a faerie standing in their midst, dressed in black and with an unpleasant smile on his lips.

"I am, although it is unfortunate it has taken so long. To change!" he said, raising his glass in a toast, and everyone roared again.

Tom needed to find Brenna and get her out of there fast. He could see only one door in the room, to the right of the fireplace. He hoped this would lead to Brenna, but to remain unseen he needed the sprites to stay clustered around the Duke in the middle of the room. He crawled, belly low to the floor, sniffing dust and grime, down the staircase, then weaved his way between the sleepers until he reached the far side of the hall, which was in deep shadow. While the planning and cheering continued, Tom crawled between the bodies which had been unceremoniously pushed up against the wall. He could feel their limbs squashing beneath him, and he tried to push them out of the way, feeling for the hard floor. Every now and again he paused and flopped, feigning sleep. Finally he was close enough to stand and slip through the doorway.

Making sure there was no one on the other side, Tom followed a corridor until he came to steps leading downwards. At the foot of the steps he stopped and looked around. The corridor was poorly lit; shadows thrown by the occasional torch snaked across the floor. The ornate decoration of the upper corridors had gone, and through half-open doors he saw storerooms housing boxes, bags of flour, jars and bottles. Eventually he came to a closed door. Trying the handle he found it was locked, but fortunately the key was still in the hole.

He pressed his ear to the door, but it was silent

within. "Brenna, are you there?" he called softly.

"Yes, yes, it's me! Tom?"

He unlocked the door.

"Tom! How did you find me?" Brenna joined him in the corridor, looking rumpled and slightly grubby, but otherwise unharmed. Her sword had gone, and she looked vulnerable without it.

"Ssh, not now. We have to get out of here." He locked the door behind them so it looked undisturbed.

"No, we can't go yet."

"What? Why not?"

"There's another prisoner, right next door. I heard them speak to him."

"Brenna, we haven't got time!"

"We can't leave him. You know we can't."

He sighed with exasperation. "But we could be caught any second!"

"We are not leaving without him. Here," she said, removing the key from the door, "I think they used the same key."

They slid the key into the lock. It turned easily.

Inside was a sleeping faerie. He was tied to a chair placed against the far wall, his body secured by coils of pale smoke that had solidified around his arms, legs and torso. He had long white-blond hair that shone with a pale light, and wore clothes that had been fine once, but which were now dirty and torn. Tom shook him gently.

The faerie's head shot up and he shouted, "Get away! How dare you touch me!" His eyes were a deep midnight blue.

Tom jumped back. "I'm here to help!" He looked anxiously at the door where Brenna waited.

"Who are you? What are you doing here?" said the faerie.

"I am *trying* to rescue you."

He shook himself awake, his eyes bright and eager. "Really? At last!" Then he looked down at the smoke wrapped solidly about him. "But I can't leave unless we can remove this restraint."

"Well we need to go now, so unless we can do this quickly we'll have to leave you here."

"These coils have to be unlocked, but I know where the key is. I have just enough power left to disguise you so you can get it for me." He looked pleadingly at Tom.

Tom glanced at the smoky restraints and wondered where a key would fit, but only asked, "Where is the key?"

"Around the neck of my treacherous rat of a brother, the Duke of Craven."

"He's your brother? I've just seen him in the hall, surrounded by murderous wood sprites! It would be impossible to get close enough."

Panic shot across the faerie's face. "I can disguise you, I promise! Please. If I don't get out of here soon he'll find out how to use the Starlight Jewel, and then he'll be too powerful for me to stop! And he'll kill me."

Tom felt his heart sinking. He just wanted to get out of here, but felt he didn't really have a choice. He looked at Brenna and she nodded. "Tom, we have to!" He grunted, not entirely seeing the "we" in this.

"If I do this I'm going to have to lock you back in the room," he said to her.

"I understand." Her face was pale but determined, and he recognised that look – it was a look that Beansprout used far too often.

8 Starfall

Tom sighed. "All right. What do I have to do?"

"As I said, the Duke has my key around his neck. It's a small key that looks like glass. It fits here." He pointed to the centre of his chest. "This binding has reduced my magic, but I can cast a spell that will draw some of this smoke to you and allow you to pass unseen into the hall. The enchantment won't last for long, but you can take the key and bring it back to me. Once I'm free I promise to get you out of here."

"How long's not long?"

"Half an hour or so?"

Tom hoped the Duke was still in the hall or he would never find him, and then he'd be captured too. "OK. Do it now."

"Come here – kneel beside me so I can reach you."

Tom knelt and the faerie pressed his index finger to Tom's forehead. He felt a strange sensation pass through him. As he looked down, he saw his body shimmering,

"What on earth …?"

"Go, quickly!"

They ran out of the door, Brenna locking it carefully behind them.

"Tom, he's right," she said, going back into the room she'd been held in. "You're barely visible. Just stick to the shadows and you'll be fine. Good luck!"

"Barely visible" wasn't reassuring, but as Brenna handed him the key he was relieved to find he could still grip things properly.

After locking Brenna in, he ran back up the corridor. It felt twice as long as before. A sprite appeared and Tom froze, but it disappeared into a store room, reappearing moments later with an armful of bottles. As the sprite went back up the stairs, Tom followed, treading softly, his heart hammering in his chest.

He edged into the hall, trying to get his breathing under control. The sprites continued to shout and sing, some aiming their spears at the far wall where several figures had been drawn. There was a rhythmical thump and cheer as the spears found their mark.

Tom saw the Duke sitting on a chair deep in the shadows cast by the balcony above. He was examining a map spread out on the table before him, in a pool of light cast by a single candle.

Tom again hugged the walls and the shadows, but nobody was even looking in his direction. He couldn't even see himself. He crept closer and closer to the Duke until he was standing behind him. It was uncanny – the Duke of Craven looked like a photographic negative of his brother. His eyes were dark and his hair was black, but with a faint dusty sheen to it, like diamond dust. He had sharper features, but they were otherwise identical.

The Duke's attention was completely on the map. Tom could see the glass key on a chain around his neck, chinking next to other, bigger keys. He flexed his fingers and tried not to breathe heavily. The Duke leaned back in his chair, closed his eyes and rubbed his face wearily with his hands. As he dropped his hands to his sides, Tom edged closer, reaching over the Duke's shoulder towards the key. The Duke's hand shot up and went to grab Tom's arm, but Tom snatched his hand back and pressed against the wall. The Duke opened his eyes and patted his shoulder, confused, then sat up and looked round, scanning the space behind him. Tom stood motionless, holding his breath.

Distracted by an approaching sprite, the Duke turned away.

"Duke, we need to go soon," said the sprite.

"Yes, all right, just give me a few more minutes. Are the horses ready?"

"I'll send someone down, they can get the girl on their way back." He strode off, shouting to one of the others.

The Duke pulled a large jewel out of his pocket. It was the size of a duck egg, and its centre glowed. He lifted it level with his eyes and gazed into it. Tom leaned forward too, peering into its depths. He thought he saw swirling stars, and leaned in closer and closer, halting abruptly as the Duke sighed, re-pocketed the jewel, and then leaned back and closed his eyes again.

Tom's stomach churned – he had to get the key now or it would all be over. He reached forward and pulled the key gently between his thumb and forefinger. The key melted off the chain and into his hands; the key recognised him.

Without hesitation he ran back across the hall, down the stairs and along the corridor. He could tell the spell was wearing off – he reckoned he had five or ten minutes' invisibility left. He heard footsteps behind him, but the sprite entered a doorway without noticing Tom.

He made it back to Brenna's room without encountering any more sprites.

"I have it," called Tom, as he and Brenna unlocked the faerie's door.

He placed the key over the spot the faerie had indicated. Magically a keyhole appeared, and the key slotted in and disappeared. There was a strange hissing sound and the smoke began to thin and disappear.

"You have no idea how good that feels!" the faerie said. Colour returned to his cheeks and he stood up gingerly. "Oh, I am so stiff!" he groaned, limping to the door, where he went to turn left.

"Not that way," Tom said. "There are hundreds of them in the hall, and some are coming any minute now to get Brenna. Is there a back way out?"

The faerie looked thoughtful. "All right, follow me. And by the way, who are you? How did a human child and another faerie arrive here?" He turned to Brenna, looking at her curiously. "Why do they want you?"

"Not now!" said Tom, giving him a gentle push. "Keep going."

The faerie frowned at him, but did as Tom suggested. They continued down passageway after passageway, twisting and turning until Tom was completely disorientated, before finally entering a larger space. In front of them was a large wooden door.

Tom tried pushing and pulling, but it wouldn't budge.

"My dear boy," said the faerie, "this is a faerie palace. It won't open just like that. Now, who are you?"

"Can't this wait?" Tom asked. "They'll discover we've gone any minute." Tom was sure he could hear voices getting louder.

The faerie smiled. "I'm not going anywhere. This is my palace and I shall have my revenge. No one knows this place better than me. They caught me by surprise last time, but not again."

"But there are hundreds of them. And we can't help any more. Our friends will be worried."

The faerie grimaced and lowered his voice to a whisper. "Don't worry, you have done more than enough. I can manage now. If I so choose, there will be endless staircases that lead nowhere; corridors that shrink to the size of a mouse hole; rooms that seal as soft and moist as a hungry mouth; doorways that lead to a howling abyss; mirrors that show your reflection then steal it and swallow you whole. They will regret ever attacking us. And he will regret ever betraying me."

As he finished, Tom saw over his shoulder two wood sprites running towards them, spears raised. Tom opened his mouth to shout a warning, but the faerie was already turning, and with a flick of his hand and a mutter of something unintelligible, the floor beneath the sprites vanished, replaced by a gaping mouth full of teeth and blood-red gums. The sprites fell in and with soft sucking noises, the mouth closed.

The faerie smiled smugly and asked, "You didn't happen to see my subjects, did you?"

"Well yes, actually," Tom said, struggling to concentrate. "They're asleep all over the floor, on the steps, in the ballroom …"

The faerie looked thoughtful. "Good. And your name?"

"Tom, and this is Brenna."

"And your friends?"

"Woodsmoke and Beansprout," Tom said impatiently, wondering why on earth that mattered.

The man bowed majestically and kissed Brenna's hand. "Madam, Sir. I am indebted. But you haven't answered my earlier question. How are you here?"

Brenna answered. "I was kidnapped by the wood sprites – I was to be given to the Queen of Aeriken."

"Some sort of exchange for her power, from what I overheard," added Tom.

"Really. She doesn't normally share her power. I wonder what's in it for her? And why you?" he mused, looking at Brenna, "and not Tom or the others?"

Brenna flushed. "I have no idea," she answered quickly. "And your name?" she asked, changing the subject.

"I am Prince Finnlugh, Bringer of Starfall and Chaos, Head of the House of Evernight. Now go, quickly. Avoid the edge of Aeriken Forest; if there's any more of them, that's where they'll be waiting."

He muttered and waved his hands, just as Woodsmoke had done under the tower, and the door opened.

Outside it was night. Tom hadn't realised they had been in the mound for so long.

The Prince added under his breath, "If ever there was a time for the King, perhaps it is now."

Tom and Brenna stopped and looked at him. "What did you say?" asked Tom.

He looked at them warily. "Nothing, ignore me."

Tom persisted. "You mentioned a king."

"I am merely thinking aloud. Forget I ever said anything."

"Well," Tom said, considering his words carefully, "we're travelling to the lake if you wish to see us again."

The Prince stared at him and then gave a slow smile.

"By the way, don't worry about being followed. I will make sure they never leave."

They stepped through the door and with a crack it shut behind them, leaving them halfway up the hill.

Tom looked at Brenna. "Thank God we're out of there. That has to be the freakiest place ever. I hope Woodsmoke doesn't live in one of those things. Are you OK?"

"Yes, apart from my shoulder. It's really sore. I fell on it when they threw that wretched net on me."

"So the Prince asked a good question. Why you? They didn't bother with the rest of us. What did they mean when they called you her 'subject'?"

Brenna glanced away, reluctant to meet Tom's eye. "I have no idea. They probably confused me with someone else. It's nothing, Tom. Just an exchange for power."

Again she changed the conversation. "Didn't you take a bit of a risk just then? The whole King thing?"

He shrugged. "It felt right."

The grass on the hill was smooth and velvety, clipped short, unlike the meadows below which were luxuriant with waist-high grasses. Once they reached the bottom, there was no sign of the main entrance. The grasses tangled around their calves and smelt fragrant and fresh. They searched for the spot where they had been attacked, hoping to pick up Woodsmoke's and Beansprout's tracks.

Keeping the river on their right, they eventually stumbled into an area of flattened grass – and the dead bodies of wood sprites. There was a moment of panic, of wondering if Woodsmoke or Beansprout lay among them, but there was no sign of either.

Tom took out his torch, holding it low over the

ground, and eventually found a faint track leading away from the mound. It was too risky to shout out, so they called in low voices: "Woodsmoke, Beansprout."

They hadn't gone far when they came across another dead sprite. They called again, and this time relief swept through Tom as Woodsmoke answered, "Tom, Brenna, is that you?" They saw a tall figure, black against the pale silver of the grass.

"Woodsmoke?" Tom shone his torch, lighting up Woodsmoke's face. "Are you OK?"

"I am, but Beansprout's not so good. How are you two?"

"We're okay. It's been … eventful," Tom answered.

They followed Woodsmoke to a ring of flattened grass. Beansprout was curled on a blanket, sleeping heavily.

"What happened?" Brenna dropped to her knees next to Beansprout, her face worried.

"She was hit in the arm by a spear. Fortunately it's only grazed, but the spear took a good chunk of skin with it. I've bound the wound, but it bled a lot and was very painful. I've given her herbs to ease the pain and help her sleep. She should be better by tomorrow, I hope."

Woodsmoke sat and Tom dropped next to him.

"How did you get out?" said Woodsmoke. "I'm sorry, I tried to get in but the magic was too strong. I thought you must be dead."

Tom related everything that happened, while Brenna curled up on the blanket next to Beansprout.

"So the Queen wants her subjects back." He looked across at Brenna, but she was silent, her eyes glinting in the starlight.

"You don't live in one of those hills, do you?" Tom

asked.

"Oh no, they are used only by the old royal tribes."

"Good, because it was really creepy. And the Prince was … odd."

Woodsmoke laughed. "Odd and powerful; I have heard many stories. Not least from my grandfather."

"Like what?"

"Another time, I think."

"Who are the other royal tribes?"

"There are quite a few, but locally there's the Duchess of Cloy's tribe, and Prince Ironroot's. Their palaces are over there." He gestured over the river. "We don't really see them any more; they hole up in their under-palaces dancing and feasting their long lives away." He stopped, lost in thought.

"And how are we getting back tomorrow, to your home?"

"We'll try to make it to the river, find a boat. It will be quicker and certainly easier. And then we go to the Isle of Avalon."

9 Vanishing Hall

The sky started to lighten, a green wash spreading across the eastern horizon. Tom had barely slept. He was cold and stiff, and was torn between going back to sleep – for days – and wanting to get moving, just to be warm. And he was very hungry. It had been hours since he'd eaten and he had only a few biscuits left.

He rummaged in his pack as Brenna stirred. Woodsmoke was gently shaking Beansprout. She woke, her face ashen in the early morning light, and struggled to sit up.

"My arm's so sore," she said, wincing as she wriggled it.

"Are you able to walk today, or do you need more rest?" said Woodsmoke.

"I'll be OK to walk, but I may not be very fast."

"I can't fly, either," said Brenna. "I hurt my shoulder yesterday. I don't want to risk it."

"We'll walk to the river, see if there's a boat we can get on. I know we're all hungry, but we should press on."

Beansprout looked over at Tom and Brenna. "I was worried we'd never see you again. How did you get out?"

Brenna laughed. "It's quite a story, we'll tell you as we walk," she said.

At about midday they reached the Little Endevorr River, a tributary of the main river they had crossed the day before. It ran slowly, its waters clear, the riverbed visible in the shallows.

They had been following it for a short time when a boat appeared, heading downstream. A man called out, "Is that you, Brenna?" Haven't seen you for a while."

Brenna waved. "Fews! How are you? I don't suppose you're taking passengers?"

"Well I don't normally, but I can make an exception for you."

He steered his boat over to the bank. It was long, like a barge, and filled with sacks and barrels. Fews was grey haired with a wrinkled brown face like an old apple. When he smiled, his eyes almost disappeared into his wrinkles, and Tom saw he'd lost most of his teeth.

"You must know Woodsmoke?" said Brenna.

"I reckon I know your face," he answered, looking Woodsmoke up and down. "You're Fahey's grandchild?"

"I am," said Woodsmoke, smiling.

"So who are these two? They don't look like they're from round here."

"They're humans, come to visit their grandfather, Jack," Brenna answered.

Tom and Beansprout said hello as they clambered into the centre of the boat and settled themselves in the gaps between the sacks.

"Oh, I see, we're having some cross-cultural relations are we? Well welcome to my boat, and don't squash anything!"

He made sure they were all settled before setting off again. "What you done to your shoulder, Brenna?"

"Had a run-in with some wood sprites by the Starfall Under-Palace."

Fews' smile disappeared. "They're getting closer, then. I hope you got rid of a few?"

"Of course. They came off worse."

"Good. There's far too many around for my liking. Don't know what's bringing them out of the forest really. Usually don't like the open."

Tom dozed in the warmth of the sun, the sacks comfortable beneath him. But every time he closed his eyes, images from the previous day raced through his mind. He could see the Prince's malevolent smile, and hear him describing what the palace could do. Once again he realised how far he was from home and how strange this place was.

His stomach rumbled, but even hunger couldn't keep him awake. Finally, he slept deeply.

He woke up when the boat changed direction and bumped the riverbank. A murmur of voices prodded his consciousness and his eyes flickered open. It was dusk and the birds called loudly, swooping over the water, black against a pale-grey sky.

He sat up and found they were surrounded by other boats, moored up and down the river around them, nudging each other in the current. They were mostly deserted, with just the odd light shining from masts and bows. On either side, high banks blocked his view beyond the river, but overhead he could see bridges crisscrossing back and forth.

Brenna and Woodsmoke stood on the riverbank talking to a short squat man who looked like a toad. He nodded a few times before hopping from view in one bound.

Tom nudged Beansprout. "Wake up madam. We're here, wherever that is."

She roused and stretched, stopping short when her

injured arm hurt. "God I'm so exhausted. I want a proper bed."

"Well, we might get one tonight, and we might find Granddad too."

She sat up quickly. "Of course, I forgot. He's going to be surprised to see us. Have you any idea where we're going now?"

"Nope, I'm just doing as I'm told."

"Well, that makes a change."

They made their way to the top of the bank where they could see their surroundings more clearly.

On either side of the river was a sprawling village, its edges melting into the twilight. There was a jumble of buildings and market stalls, several running alongside the river. Walkways and bridges linked the buildings and spanned the river, some high above the ground. Lights twinkled in the dusk. Strange-looking people were milling around, and music and singing drifted through the air. Tempting scents mingled and beckoned; Tom could smell food. His mouth watered.

Woodsmoke called them over to where he stood at the crossroads of the road and a bridge. "I'm borrowing a horse and cart to take us home; we should be there by midnight." He looked tired but pleased, and ran his hand through his long hair. He had unslung his bow and it rested at his feet while he flexed his shoulders up and down. Brenna stood next to him, deep in thought as she gazed across the village and the surrounding countryside.

"So where are we?" Beansprout asked.

"Endevorr Village. And that," Woodsmoke pointed across the river, "is Vanishing Wood, where we live."

"That's great. I'm starving. Can we get some food?"

Tom asked.

Beansprout nodded. "Me too! Please don't make me wait."

"All right," said Woodsmoke. "I'm pretty hungry myself. We have a while before the cart arrives."

They strolled across to the nearest stalls and gazed at the displays of food. There was a big roast pig turning on a spit, the fat hissing as it dripped onto the fire; plates full of pies and pastries, and dishes of fruit that looked sweet and juicy.

"I want it all," Tom said, drooling.

"I'll get you some pies," said Woodsmoke. "Trust me, they're good!" He handed over some money and received a tray of thick crust pies in return. They tucked in, groaning with pleasure.

Distracted by the rumbling of wheels, Tom looked around and saw a horse and cart being driven by the short toad-like man he'd seen before. He hopped down and threw the reins at Woodsmoke, saying in a gruff voice, "See you sometime tomorrow then, Woodsmoke. Safe journey."

He took little interest in the rest of them and headed off over the bridge, the strange lollop in his walk making the curve of his upper spine more noticeable.

They bought some more food for the journey, then Woodsmoke jumped up onto the front of the cart and grabbed the reins. The others climbed into the back, snuggling under blankets.

They trundled along the road next to the river, but while Brenna slept, Tom and Beansprout were wide awake, staring at everything around them. Small lanes tunnelled between the buildings, burrowing into the heart of the village. They were full of strange beings hurrying about their business. The people – or rather faeries, Tom corrected himself – looked like something out of a story book. Some were tall and stately, and glided along without appearing to walk. Most of them had long hair, which the women wore elaborately braided and piled on top of their heads.

There were also little people that looked like pixies, olive skinned and sharp featured, as well as creatures that were half-animal, half-human. A man with the enormous ears of a hare walked past, and Tom thought he saw a satyr down by the river.

Eventually they passed out of the village and into woodland, where the twilight thickened and midges rose in clouds. The crowds thinned, and before long all they could hear was the jingle of the reins and the clomp of hooves.

They travelled for several hours before turning off on to a road that led into thicker woodland. It was now deep night, and the starlight was blocked by the canopy of leaves. Occasionally Tom saw flickering lights in the distance, but they quickly disappeared before he could work out what they were. Then, at last, a mass of golden lights appeared through the trees.

They entered a clearing containing a well, and a grassy area on which several horses were grazing. Lanterns hung from the trees, illuminating a rambling building of wood and stone that spread in a semi-circle around them. Assorted towers sprouted out of it, some short and squat, others tall and spindly, piercing the canopy high overhead. Vast tree trunks lay at angles to form part of the buildings, and rooms seemed suspended in the branches. It was the oddest collection of buildings Tom had ever seen, and they looked as if they would topple down at any minute.

Woodsmoke directed the horse through an archway

into a courtyard, and jumped down, the rest of them following. A door at the base of one of the corkscrew towers flew open and a figure strode out saying, "Who's there? We're not expecting guests."

"Well we're not guests! It's me, Woodsmoke, with Brenna and a couple of friends."

"Oh the Gods – you're back! We were wondering what was taking you so long." The figure strode into view and Tom saw an older faerie with feathered eyebrows and a shock of white hair shot through with red. He trailed sparks, and thick black smoke billowed out of the doorway behind him.

"Are you burning the place down, Father?" Woodsmoke asked.

"No, just experimenting. Have a little faith," he said. "My my my, so you've brought Jack's grandchildren. How very pleased I am to meet you." He shook their hands and reached to kiss Brenna on both cheeks. His hand was firm and dry and he smelt of gunpowder. His clothes were patched and ripped and speckled with burns and singed edges, and across his cheek was a smear of a grey glittery substance. There was a wild distraction in his eyes; he looked as if he wasn't quite all there.

"Well, I'm glad you're back. Your grandfather's somewhere in the main house," he said, striding back towards the tower. "I'll leave you to it!"

"Typical," muttered Woodsmoke. "He's more interested in his experiments than in what's happening anywhere else. You go ahead, I'll sort the horse and see you in a minute."

They followed Brenna into the house and across a huge high-ceilinged kitchen lit only by a smouldering fire.

They wound their way through room after room and up several stairways inside tree trunks, before coming out into a big square room dimly lit by candles.

Tom saw two figures in front of the fire. One was standing with his arms outstretched, as if performing to an audience. The other sat watching and listening. They were both so absorbed that Tom hesitated to interrupt; instead the three of them listened at the door as the man who was standing said, "And he flung his club so far and so high that he knocked a star from the sky. The star skittered across the night sky leaving a blazing trail of light behind it until, gathering speed, it fell to earth."

And then they were spotted, and the man sitting in the chair jumped to his feet and shouted, "Tom! Beansprout! What are you doing here?" He was already trotting across the room, arms outstretched and a big grin on his face. "I thought I'd never see you again!"

Tom and Beansprout ran across the room to meet him, and he crushed them in bear hugs. Tom felt himself become shaky, and had an urge to sit down. He could hardly believe that Granddad was actually here.

"Hello Fahey," said Brenna, greeting the other man with a half-hug, betraying the injury to her shoulder.

Tom's grandfather turned to Fahey, his eyes bright and his voice slightly breathless. "My grandchildren, they're here!"

"Well I can see that, Jack. I'm not blind! What are we all standing for? Come on, sit down and tell us why you're here. Longfoot!" he yelled. "Bring us drinks and snacks."

After a bustle of moving chairs they sat around the fire and looked at each other, a silence falling momentarily as they all wondered where to start. Jack spoke first. "So why –

and how – are you here?"

"Perhaps we shouldn't start there." Beansprout winced slightly. "It's sort of an accident. But how are *you*? And how did *you* get here?" He looked so well that she added, "You look great!"

"I am, I am! But you've grown since I last saw you, and it's only been a few months."

"Longer than that, Granddad," she said. "It's been over a year!"

Jack looked open-mouthed at Fahey who shrugged and said, "I told you so."

Tom hadn't wanted to criticise, but seeing his grandfather all warm and happy in front of the fire made him suddenly cross. "We've been really worried about you! How could you just go?"

Jack looked stricken. "I'm sorry, Tom. I realise it seems thoughtless, but at the time it felt like the right thing to do."

"But how? Why? Didn't you think we'd be worried?"

"That's why I left the note." Panic crossed his face. "You did see the note, didn't you?"

"Yes we did, but it was still odd!"

Beansprout interrupted. "Tom, maybe we should talk about this later?" She turned to Jack and smiled. "It's so good to see you! I swear you look younger!"

Tom was still fuming, but he bit his tongue. He realised Beansprout was right – Granddad did look younger, almost fresher.

"It's the air in this place, it does marvellous things to you. I've learnt to ride a horse!"

"Have you? That's so exciting! And you live here?" said Beansprout.

"He certainly does," said Fahey. "He helps me with my storytelling."

Tom looked at Fahey with dislike. He was about to say something to him when he saw Beansprout glaring, so he continued to sit in silence.

Beansprout turned to Fahey and asked, "So is that what you do, tell stories?"

"I do. I am a bard, and a very good one," he said proudly. He had a noble face with silver hair that was combed and shining and tied back in a ponytail secured by a black ribbon.

"Oh he is – and what stories!" said Jack. "Tom, you'd love them." He smiled nervously, as if fearing another outburst. Tom looked at him in stony silence.

While the others talked, Tom fumed. This wasn't the reunion he'd hoped for. He'd expected his grandfather to be worn out and tired, desperate to return home – but he didn't look desperate at all.

Longfoot arrived, a plump faerie in a long frock coat, with a face that was a little mouse-like. His nose twitched ever so slightly, and he had long quivering whiskers arching over a small pink mouth. He carried a large tray on which were crowded glasses of wine and pots of tea, and a pile of toast and butter, which they all tucked into with relish – even Tom who, although grumpy, was still starving.

When Woodsmoke arrived they told Jack and Fahey about their journey. It was a chaotic, much-interrupted story, but before they could tell them about the Lady of the Lake, Woodsmoke said, "Enough. It's late. Everyone's tired, and two of us are injured, so we should go to bed. We can continue this tomorrow." He said this with such finality and authority that no one argued.

Longfoot was summoned, and Tom and Beansprout were escorted to bedrooms, somewhere in the cavernous house.

10 Old Tales

The house was old and ramshackle with warmth that seemed to ooze out of the walls. It creaked and moaned unexpectedly, and seemed to mutter to itself, which gave Tom a restless night full of vivid dreams that chased themselves around and around in his head.

His grumpiness was still apparent the next morning. He brooded and scowled as Longfoot escorted them through the confusion of rooms to the first-floor breakfast room, perched in the leafy branches of a large oak.

"Stop it, Tom," hissed Beansprout. "You're behaving like a child."

He ignored her and picked up a plate, loading it with a large breakfast from the selection laid out on the sideboard.

It wasn't long before Fahey and Jack arrived. Beansprout gave her grandfather a kiss on the cheek, but Tom just grumbled a greeting under his breath. No one else seemed to notice his bad mood; they started chatting without him, Beansprout asking about the house and why they lived in the middle of the wood.

Fahey took a last bite of scrambled egg and buttery toast, sighed contentedly and said, "Can I tell you The Tale of Vanishing Hall?"

Tom rolled his eyes, but Beansprout, remembering how mesmerising his story had been the previous night, said, "Yes please!"

Fahey began. "Once upon a time there lived a count – Count Slipple – one of the fey who lived in the under-palace of the House of Evernight. The under-palace was a warren of vast halls, twisted corridors and shadowy rooms, hidden under the earth in a great grassy mound. Time moved differently in this place, slipping quickly like ghosts through walls, and all of its inhabitants were as old as the earth that buried them, although by a quirk of their race their skin looked as smooth and fresh as thick cream.

"One day, Count Slipple had a terrible argument with Prince Vastness, the head of the House of Evernight. Prince Vastness was powerful and vengeful, and his words carried great power, but Count Slipple was stronger than the Prince realised. Years of resentment rose between them and their words spat back and forth like fireworks. The air steamed and hissed, and fiery barbs and stings snatched at their skin and scorched their hair, until their clothes hung from them in tatters. Grand faerie noblemen, ladies and courtiers ran shrieking into dark hollows and hidden corners as the air crackled with harmful intent. Eventually the evil in their words manifested into a great black tornado before which Count Slipple ran for his life.

"He fled to the stables deep below the under-palace and, flinging himself upon his horse, he whispered the magic words. The hillside rumbled opened above him, starlight pouring through. He raced across the plains and into the tangled woods, pursued by black stallions carrying Prince Vastness and his royal guard. Branches whipped his face and grabbed at his clothes until, in the middle of the woods, he fell from his horse. Exhausted and injured he lay face down in the oil-dark earth, the slime of autumn leaves crushed beneath him, the scent of decay heavy in his nostrils. The ground thundered with the hooves of the pursuing horses and he realised if they found him, he would die.

"Inches from his eyes he saw an acorn resting on the forest floor, and he imagined how warm and safe he would feel in such a small tidy space. As the wild screams of the stallions grew closer he reached for the acorn, and holding it in his hand, whispered, 'I wish, I wish, I wish.'

"The next thing he knew, he was cushioned in a cocoon of velvety blackness. He could still feel the thudding of the black stallions and the ground shook beneath him, but he was warm and content. The thundering hooves fell silent, replaced by the taunts and threats of the riders, which carried menacingly across the still glade. He lay there for what seemed like hours, maybe days, exhausted and weak, sometimes sleeping, other times thinking and regretting.

"Eventually, when he felt better, and when the percussion of hooves and voices had ceased, replaced by the murmur of wind and rain and the creep of roots beneath him, he decided it was time to leave his cocoon. He thought he would wish himself out of it as he had wished himself in, but however hard he tried, nothing happened. Frustrated, he shouted and cursed and uttered magical incantations, but his howls were swallowed by his prison.

"He tried another way, pushing against his boundaries with his fingers, toes, hands, feet, elbows, knees, shoulders and head, and as he pushed he grew and grew, and the acorn grew with him. It was exhausting work, but slowly a crack appeared in the shell of the acorn and light glinted in the Count's eyes; a gleam of gold in the velvety blackness that dazzled his light-bewildered gaze.

"Eventually there came a time when he stopped growing, but the acorn didn't. It grew around him until it was the size of a room, and the crack in the acorn was the size of his arm; a slice of silver pierced the space, cutting the floor in two.

"The Count lay and gathered his strength, admiring the rippled walls that looked like the surface of water. He thought that, as he had no place to live, it would make a fine house and would hide him from those seeking to find him. But he was hungry and needed food, so he made the crack wider and wider until he could step out, and found himself where he had fallen earlier.

"He stood under the glow of the moon. Seeing soft green foliage all around, he realised he had lain in the acorn for months. He heard an insistent splash and, walking a small distance, saw a spring bubbling up from the ground. In the distance, deer were grazing. His horse had long since disappeared.

"Smiling, he looked back at the now giant acorn and saw that it was continuing to grow, roots pushing beneath the ground with blind urgency. Its roof was arched and branches grew from its rounded sides, contorting and twisting into towers that shot vertically upwards, reaching to the stars. The walls were as shiny as a polished apple and slivers of light slid across its curved walls like a smile.

"The Count slipped through the shadows of the tangled wood, his footfall soft on the ground. He looked for signs that the Prince or his men might still be watching, and he was wary of traps in the undergrowth. But apart from the hoots of owls, the wood was silent. He walked as far as the edge of the wood, and gazing across the plains saw the grassy mound in the distance; an absence against the dark night sky. He sighed, knowing he could never return there.

"He walked back across the forest as the ground mist

rose and the trees announced themselves in the pale dawn light; beeches and oaks that locked branches against intruders but which, recognising him as their own, let him pass with an unravelling whisper before knotting themselves thickly in his wake. Bird calls rose in a mass, and soon he walked through an ever-increasing crescendo of noise back to the acorn that had sheltered him.

So Count Slipple turned his back on the under-palace and became Lord Vanishing, and the acorn became Vanishing Hall. In time he took a wife and had many children, grandchildren and great-grandchildren, and it wasn't until he was on his deathbed that he told them who he really was, and what lay beneath the great green mound in the distance.

"And all of his descendants lived to an uncanny old age. Their skin had a creamy whiteness, their eyes a vivid greenness that captured the fruitfulness of the forest, and their tempers were as vicious as the summer storms that lit the landscape with the unexpected flash and sizzle of lightening."

By the time Fahey had finished his tale he was standing, waving his arms around, his face animated and excited.

"So this house is from that acorn?" said Beansprout. "That's so amazing!"

Even Tom had to admit that was interesting.

Woodsmoke, who had walked in unnoticed, so engrossed were they in the story, said, "Are you telling tall tales again, Grandfather?"

Fahey looked slightly put out. "It's not a tall tale, and I shall show you the original room later." He turned to Beansprout and Tom. "It's slightly damp now so we don't use it much any more. Obviously it's been built on over the years, bits added by different generations, but it's essentially the same place, and every now and then a new tower will sprout or an old one will collapse. It's a wonderful place to live. In fact, when I was away the old spindle tower completely disappeared." He sighed and a shadow briefly fell across his face. "I missed this place when I was away."

Jack patted his shoulder. "Don't think of that time, Fahey. You're back now."

"Talking of old tales," said Woodsmoke, "we have something to tell you. Tom met the Lady of the Lake, and she gave him a job to do."

Fahey slapped the table and looked at Woodsmoke with ill-concealed hunger, and a touch of wariness. "He met who? What did she want?"

"He has to wake the King."

"No!" Jack interrupted immediately. "He will not. I won't have him put in danger. He shouldn't even be here, Woodsmoke. It's your fault he's here."

Tom was shocked at his grandfather's outburst. What did he know that made him think it was dangerous? He looked at Woodsmoke, wondering what he would say, but Woodsmoke nodded saying, "Tell them what happened, Tom."

There was an air of expectancy, as if they knew something that he didn't, but he told them of his encounter in the Greenwood and what the wood sprites were threatening in the House of Evernight. He ended by saying, "I don't think I have much choice. And besides, Prince Finnlugh, Bringer of Starfall and Chaos might be able to help."

"Well well well." There was a fire burning in Fahey's

eyes now. "You can't rely on the old Royal Houses, Tom. They have their own interests. But show me the silver twig."

Tom still felt a bit resentful of Fahey's friendship with his grandfather, and now of his interference with his task, so he shrugged and said, "I haven't got it now. It's in my room."

Fahey looked at him thoughtfully. "All right, I'll have a look later. But Tom, don't underestimate how hard this will be, even with this silver twig – which, by the way, is probably a powerful charm giving you some protection as you travel through this realm."

"How do you know it's a dangerous task?" Tom snapped.

"Because I tried to wake him myself, and was imprisoned for decades for my efforts!" Fahey looked annoyed.

"But that's because it wasn't meant to happen then. Now it is. She imprisoned you, but she told me it was time."

Jack intervened. "I still don't want you doing this. This isn't your fight."

"Actually," said Woodsmoke, "it is now. You don't refuse the Lady of the Lake. And besides, apparently he's related."

"To whom?" asked Fahey.

"The King."

"How can he possibly be related to King Arthur?" Jack spluttered.

"Because she said so! And I don't know how!" Tom yelled.

"I don't care if you are. You are not doing this," persisted Jack.

Fahey smiled grimly. "It isn't a case of what we want,

Jack. The best thing we can do is to help. It will take a few days' riding to get to the Isle, and we can go too. In fact, the sooner we go the better. I presume you'll come?"

Jack looked across at Beansprout. "I suppose you'll go too? Even though I don't want you to."

"Sorry, Granddad, but yes." She looked sheepish as she added, "You came here without asking anyone!"

Tom glared at him. "Yes, you did."

Jack pushed away from the table and paced around the room, running his hands through his hair just as Tom did when he was thinking. He muttered to himself, "Well it's a fine example I gave, I suppose."

"You did say you wanted adventure, Jack," said Fahey.

Jack turned to Tom, now very annoyed. "Tom, this wouldn't have happened if you hadn't come. I told you I was fine. Why doesn't anybody ever listen to me?"

"Well, you can be sure I won't bother again!" Tom yelled as he marched out of the door.

Jack yelled after him. "Well you're stuck with me for now, because I'm coming too!"

Tom retrieved the charm from his room and left the house.

"So what are you so grumpy about?"

Tom turned to see Woodsmoke following him. He shrugged. "Nothing, I'm fine."

"You are not fine, you're sulking like a child."

Tom glared at him. "Well you're not the one who's travelled here to find his grandfather, only to find he's not even been missed!"

"Oh, so that's what this is all about!" Woodsmoke looked at Tom in puzzlement.

Tom ignored him and headed towards what he

presumed were the stables. He could hear the horses snickering and he smelt sweet hay and manure. In the far corner was the twisted tower where Woodsmoke's father lived. It was a beautiful day; cool in the shade but hot in the sun. The sky was blue and the trees were flush with bright green leaves. It was difficult to believe they were somewhere other than the world he was so familiar with. He looked at the silver bough in his hands and felt the world tilt slightly. This was not familiar. He was in a strange place being asked to do things he didn't quite understand. It was supposed to be simple – find Granddad and go home. His resentment grew – he was having to do something for people he didn't really know, and for a place that wasn't his home.

He wheeled round and shouted to Woodsmoke. "Actually, I don't see why I should have to do this." He waved the bough in the air. "We've found Granddad, and he doesn't seem that bothered to see us. I may as well go home. All this," he gestured wildly at everything, "is not my problem."

"I thought you wanted to help? She asked you – specifically you!"

"I did, but now I don't." Tom stared fiercely at Woodsmoke, his anger now obvious. "I've changed my mind, and I'm sick of being here. Just leave me alone – I don't want to talk about it anymore." He turned his back and strode off. He had no idea where he was going and he didn't care.

Tom's angry thoughts led him out beyond the stables, where he meandered through the trees. Here they were well-spaced, like trees in a park. He found a large flat rock, beyond which was a tangled thicket of trees. This must be the boundary of Woodsmoke's land. He lay on the rock sunning himself, mulling over the disaster of finally being reunited with Granddad.

His thoughts were interrupted by a voice calling some way behind him. It was Beansprout, sounding forlorn.

"Tom, where are you? It's me."

He ignored her, hoping she wouldn't see him and would go away.

She shouted again. She was getting closer. He lay still, hoping the silver twig gave him powers of invisibility, when suddenly she spoke right next to him, making him jump.

"Tom, stop ignoring me. I've come to see if you're okay. Are you?"

"As you can see, I'm fine," he said, refusing to look at her.

She shuffled herself into a spot next to him on the rock, and he reluctantly gave way.

"What do you want?"

"Oh, aren't you gracious? Like I said, I've come to see if you're all right. Woodsmoke said you'd marched off in a strop. He thinks you're crazy. I explained this is normal for you. What's the matter?"

"Nothing. I've just had enough and it's time to go." He looked anywhere but at her.

"But you've been given a task—"

"Who cares about the task?" Tom interrupted. "Why should you care, why should I? This isn't our world or our problem. It's theirs."

"Well, that will make Granddad happy, at least. He didn't want you to do it."

Tom snorted with impatience. "Like that's supposed to make it so much better? He doesn't care that we're here anyway."

"That's not true and you know it!" Beansprout shot back. "Although it would help if you'd actually speak to him. We've travelled all this way and you've barely looked at him!"

"Well it hardly looks like he's missed us. Look where he's living!"

"Isn't that a good thing? What kind of people would we be if we wanted him to be miserable?"

Tom glared into the distance, saying nothing.

"Seriously, Tom, what did you think would happen?"

Tom remained silent.

"I don't think he'll be coming back with us. You know that, right? If he's going to stay here, shouldn't we make sure it's safe for him? If we can?"

"No!" Tom replied, finally. "If he decides to stay he'll have to cope with whatever happens, wood sprites or not! That's his choice, just like it was his choice to come here."

Beansprout sighed. "Why do you always get like this?"

"Get like what?" he snapped.

"Get sulky when what happens in your head doesn't happen in real life."

"I do not get sulky."

"You do it all the time."

Tom didn't reply, trying to ignore the little voice inside telling him it was true.

Beansprout sat looking at the side of Tom's head. "I'd do it, using your twig thingy, but she didn't ask me," she said, a note of regret in her voice.

Tom pulled the little silver twig out of his pocket. He'd put it there meaning to show Jack and Fahey. He turned it slowly in his hands.

For the first time since Beansprout had sat down,

Tom turned and looked at her properly. He scratched absently at the sole of his trainer as he spoke. "I don't know what I want to do – or anything, really."

For a few minutes they sat in silence, then Beansprout pushed her hair back behind her ears, saying, "So what's the plan? Are we going home?"

He continued to pick at his shoe and sighed. "No, I suppose we'll stay."

"And are you going to speak to Granddad – properly?"

He narrowed his eyes at her. "Don't nag, it's unattractive."

"Well don't wait too long then, or I will!" And with that she slipped off the rock and started walking back, a smile of triumph on her face.

Tom didn't yet feel ready to return to the hall. He lay on the rock feeling its warmth beneath him and the sun on his face, and wondered what he really *had* expected once he got here. He hadn't thought beyond finding Jack. He'd assumed Jack must be in trouble, even though his note said he wasn't, because Tom couldn't imagine why he'd want to leave. He groaned inwardly. Why didn't he think about things more? Oh well, too late now. He was here and he had a sort of job to do, and he had no idea why he'd been asked to do it. Why hadn't he asked more questions at the time? Instead he'd sat there blankly, just nodding, without a clue what it was all about. In fact, the only one who seemed to know anything was Fahey, and Tom had been so rude to him. He groaned again. Now he was going to have to go back and be pleasant and apologise for behaving like an ass.

But he wanted to put that moment off for a while, so

he continued to lie on the rock, eyes closed against the sun, holding the bough loosely in his hands.

Hearing noises, he sat up and looked around, thinking there was someone there … but he was alone. After another cautious scan of his surroundings, he lay down and closed his eyes again. He could hear the wind in the treetops; it sounded like voices, a soft muttering of encouragement to the leaves to grow. He could hear the movement of small creatures in the earth below him, and something that felt like a pulse, like hearing his own blood moving through his body. He could feel the bough, warm beneath his fingers. A sudden image shot into his mind, of an island: fields of fruit trees, golden wheat, flowers and bees, and in the centre a large, dark, deep cave. He felt dread in the pit of his stomach, like a nightmare, and opened his eyes again quickly to chase away the image. He hoped it wasn't what he thought it was.

11 The Hidden Isle

The shadows around them lengthened and the air grew cool as the day drew to a close. A chill wind blew, carrying the smell of rain and wet earth across the tufts of springy grass and purple and yellow heathers that covered the moor. Huge rocks, blunt and misshapen, rose from the ground, some big enough to offer shelter. Ahead of them was the massive granite formation of Fell Tor.

They had been travelling for well over a week, climbing to the higher ground of the moor. Vanishing Wood, and the neighbouring Fret Woods, were far behind them and the summery weather had also gone. Tom was aching, cold and saddle-sore. No matter how many layers he wore, the wind seemed to find its way through them, and it wasn't until they sheltered at night he could even begin to get warm.

Night brought its own problems. The wind carried howls, whispers and threats. The fire they huddled around gave off only a meagre amount of light, as if the surrounding darkness was sucking it up. After nightfall, the ground mist rose and ghostly figures appeared, standing just beyond the edge of the firelight, watching and listening. When they emerged, Tom felt the hair on the back of his neck prickle, and goosebumps rise along his skin. Woodsmoke, Brenna and Fahey took little notice of the watchers, but Tom, Beansprout and Jack were nervous and slept badly, even though they had a night watch.

Beansprout had asked if the watchers were real.

"Of course they are," Fahey had said, "although they can't touch you – they're not real in the sense that we are. They are–" he'd leaned forward for emphasis, raising his feathered eyebrows, "your guilty thoughts, brought to life by the dark night."

"They're what?" Beansprout had asked, her face alarmed and confused.

"Every little lie, harsh word or unfair judgement," Fahey had said, shaking his head. "They're out there, watching."

For a moment they had all looked beyond the light of the fire, wondering what they had done that caused a figure to be standing there, watching, before quickly dropping their eyes to the fire again.

However, today Tom was so tired he knew he'd sleep well tonight, regardless of who or what the figures were. The party aimed for the foot of the tor where there was a cave offering proper shelter. From there it was another half a day's ride to the lake.

Tom adjusted his position behind Brenna. A horse had to be the most uncomfortable method of transport. There were four horses and six riders; he was sharing a ride, as was Beansprout behind Woodsmoke. His grandfather, however, looked very comfortable on his horse.

Tom tried to adjust his movements to the horse's, but failed miserably. He gave up and bumped along painfully.

They dismounted at the base of Fell Tor and, lighting torches, inspected the interior of the cave. It was large and dry with plenty of room for them to spread out. After satisfying himself that there were no hidden exits, Woodsmoke unpacked the food and Tom built the fire. When it was burning steadily he called to Woodsmoke, "I'm going to walk up the tor to join the others."

The wind blew fiercely as he rounded the rough path that circled the tor, and he pulled his clothes tightly around him. About halfway up he found the others sheltering in a hollow. They were looking at the silver shine of the lake in the distance, a shine that stopped abruptly as it met the mist dividing the lake.

"That mist never goes," Fahey said. "No matter how hot the day, it's always impossible to see the island in the centre."

"Are you sure it has an island?" Jack asked.

"Well, so the old tales say."

"Has anyone tried to land on it?"

"It's impossible to sail anywhere on that lake. You think you're making headway and then the shore's back in front of you again. I tried for hours, only to end up back where I started. Until of course … Boom! I was suddenly trapped in a tree." He didn't look at them, his attention wrapped up in the lake and the past.

"Are you feeling OK?" Beansprout asked.

"Strange memories, that's all."

The moor below them was desolate, its wide expanses of wind-flattened greenery relieved only by blunt-headed rocks rising like whales from the earth.

Down by the lake edge Tom saw a circle of standing stones. They must be huge, he thought, because even from here they were an impressive sight. The circle reminded him of Stonehenge.

Perhaps it was something to do with the tor, but that

night, the watchers seemed to Tom to be stronger, more visible, as if they insisted on being acknowledged. They had built the fire as close to the cave entrance as they could without smoking themselves out. The flames flickered and obscured the view of the moor beyond them, but still Tom could see the watchers.

While they ate, they sat close to the fire, piling on wood so that the flames climbed steadily higher. But as they settled down to sleep, they all crept to the back of the cave and sheltered behind bags and blankets. Woodsmoke had said they wouldn't see the watchers after tonight, as they wouldn't venture close to the lake. Tom could hear the horses snuffling and shuffling unconcerned outside, and wished he could ignore the visitors too.

They came upon the circle at midday, when the stones' shadows were at their shortest. The stones looked as if they had stood there for centuries, solid and unyielding to the weather and the passage of time. Carvings jostled for space on every stone, reminding Tom of the carvings under Mishap Folly at home. In the centre of the ring was a smooth floor of white stone.

They walked around and between the stones, their fingers tracing the carvings, the stone cold beneath their touch. The shoreline of the lake was a short distance away, fringed by a narrow beach of sand sculpted by wind and waves. Now they were closer to the lake they could see that the mist rose up like a wall across the water.

Tom walked to the water's edge. The others joined him, forming a straggling line along the beach. As they gazed across the water Tom turned to them. "What now?"

Fahey pointed to the mist. "Someone's coming."

A long, narrow boat slipped out of the mist, gliding

through the water without a ripple. The curved bronze peak of its prow rose high above them, topped by a roaring dragon figurehead, its fierce eyes glaring across the water. A huge square sail stretched across the middle of the boat, filled with wind, even though there wasn't so much as a breeze blowing. Eventually the boat stopped a short distance from the shore.

Tom felt a thrill of anticipation. No one spoke. They stood rapt, as silent and still as statues.

The Lady of the Lake stepped into view on the bow. She looked regal and imposing with her long silver hair flowing around her shoulders and across her vivid green dress. She raised her arm and pointed at them.

Tom felt his head tighten as if there was a band around it, and a soft voice spoke directly in his head. He stumbled and fell to his knees, his hands clutching his head.

Beansprout rushed to his side. "Tom, are you all right?"

"I can hear her, *right in here*. Can't you? Damn! It didn't hurt like this the other day."

"No, I can't hear anything. What's she saying?" Beansprout turned to glare at the woman who stood pointing at Tom. "Stop it!" she yelled at her. "You're hurting him!"

The others remained motionless, gazing towards the boat.

"I don't think she meant to hurt me, it's OK." Tom's face eased and he straightened up. "She wants me to go with her."

"Go where?"

"Where do you think? The island in the lake!"

"On your own? What about me? Ow!" Beansprout

clutched her head too.

"What did she say?" Tom asked, guessing what had caused the pain.

"She told me to wait."

"Well then, I'd better go." He smiled nervously at Beansprout and added, "Wish me luck."

He walked across the narrow beach and into the water, every step taking him deeper, until the water lapped his thighs. When he reached the boat he grabbed the side and hauled himself over. As soon as Tom's feet touched the deck the boat started to move, back towards the mist. The sail flapped and turned, and the shoreline disappeared.

The mist pressed into his skin, eyes and hair. Every time he breathed in, moisture rushed into his mouth and lungs, until he felt saturated. Beads of water formed on the hairs on the back of his hands. His jeans were already soaked through and he shivered in the cold. The ends of the ship were invisible, and he couldn't even see the water.

The Lady of the Lake had gone and he stood alone. Seeking shelter, he looked for a hatch in the deck, but saw nothing except wet planks of wood. It was very un-boat-like. There were no stores or ropes, no helm or anchor.

He shrugged off his backpack and took out a fleece. He didn't change his wet jeans, thinking he may have to wade into the water again when they reached the next shore – if there was one.

He couldn't even detect movement. There was no wind, no sign of rippling water, no noise of any kind that might indicate where land was. For all he knew he was motionless, stranded in the middle of the lake, freezing to death.

At least his head felt better now her voice was out of

it. He tried to remember her exact words, but struggled, as if he had heard them a long time ago. Well he knew *what* he had to do, just not *how*.

He decided it was pointless to keep standing. No matter how hard he looked, the mist was impenetrable, so he sat with his back against the mast, his pack in the small of his back, closed his eyes and tried to rest.

Tom was awoken by the boat scraping across the ground. He had no idea how long he'd been asleep for. He was cold and stiff, and it was only with difficulty that he pushed himself up off the deck to see where he was.

The mist had cleared to reveal a pale blue sky, although tendrils still ribboned through the air and wrapped themselves about the rocks on the shore in front of him. Gnarled trees lined the beach, and beyond were steep hills thickly clad in tangled trees and bushes. On the summit of the highest hill was a stand of trees, light trickling through the gaps. To the right, a narrow crevasse punctured the smooth line of the hills.

He was utterly alone. The only sound was of an unseen bird calling high above, its cry eerie and forlorn, emphasising his solitude. The waves hushed insistently against the shingle, and Tom realised he was going to have to get wet again.

He slid over the side of the boat and waded to the shore, then tried to squeeze the water out of his jeans, telling himself, "It's not cold, you're just imagining it." He debated building a fire, but curiosity drew him onwards, away from the shore towards the break in the hills.

The shingle slid beneath his feet, making his movements awkward, but once he entered the crevasse the ground flattened and hardened. The shadowed sides were cushioned with moss and dripping with slime and trickling water. The sky was a narrow band of blue high above him, and his footsteps echoed as he walked further in.

After a while the path climbed and curled around the hill. The undergrowth was dense and crowded the path, and he began to sweat with the effort of the climb. Finally he emerged into a clearing and saw a broad vale below, filled with fertile fields, green meadows and trees. It was the scene from the dream he'd had on the flat rock, and although it was beautiful, his stomach tightened with dread. On the far side of the vale he made out a long low building of golden stone, glowing in the sunlight, while in the centre was a rocky hill and the dark mouth of a cave. Tom sank on to the sandy path, drank from a bottle of water and wondered what to do.

The light was falling, the sun sinking rapidly, the sky turning from pale blue to smoky violet. Stars appeared, brighter and closer to him than they had ever been before.

Below him in the vale the woman appeared beneath the trees. She gazed up at him and he felt a gentle push inside his head, before she turned and walked towards the cave.

"OK, so you want me to follow you? I get it," Tom muttered, and he scrambled to his feet and down the path.

The valley was silent. Odd shapes appeared at the edges of his vision, and although he turned quickly, he saw only shadows of an uncertain size and shape. The woman flitted like a ghost, always just ahead of him, through the soft twilight. No matter how he hurried, he couldn't seem to get closer. Arriving at the cave, she stepped in and disappeared.

Tom jogged to keep up with her and arrived breathing heavily. He stopped at the threshold and peered into the murky gloom. She waited in the shadows beyond a small fire burning in the centre. To the left was a cavernous hole, and Tom could see the start of a narrow staircase descending into the blackness.

He took a few steps. "What is this place?"

For the first time she actually spoke, and her voice was odd, like wind chimes. "It's the place where things end, rest, wait, and watch."

"And why am I here?"

"Tom, you know why! You have to wake the King."

"Why? What for?"

"He has to stop the Queen. She is destroying everything. He must go to the old forest."

She had the most maddening way of talking, as if he should know this.

"But why me? Why blood? And how do you know? You might be making it up!"

"Merlin insisted that whoever woke Arthur must be related by blood. It was one of his conditions during our negotiations, and so it was woven into the spell."

Before he could speak, images appeared in Tom's mind. An old man and a young woman, sitting around a fire at the edge of the lake, under a star-filled sky. Between them a long silver sword, flashing with firelight and shadow. The old man shouting, "Vivian! I insist. If he must awake here, he must not be alone. One of his kin must wake him."

"You are a sentimental old fool. He will not be alone!"

"If you deny this request, I deny you him!"

"And I keep the sword."

He softens. "Please, he is like my son."

She hesitates and eventually nods. "Then his

descendants will be marked, and I shall follow them all." She reaches into a bag at her side and pulls out herbs and a small cauldron, and together they start to chant.

Tom shook his head and blinked. "Was that you? You're Vivian?"

"A very young me."

"But you aren't one of them. The fey. What are you?"

"I am human, like you. I dedicated my life to magic and decided to stay here, a very long time ago. I helped negotiate the sword."

"But why me?" he insisted.

"I followed all of you. Some of you are too old, some too young, some too weak. Who sent Fahey to your world, Tom? Who did he bring here? Who followed? Was it chance? Luck? Design? And you have the mark, do you not? A dark sword-shaped birthmark across your arm."

Again he had a feeling of being out of his depth; a pawn in someone else's game. His hand moved subconsciously over the top of his right arm, over the long birthmark, and he remembered his mother's mark and wondered if either of her parents had had one too. "How do you know that?"

"I put it there."

He had a sudden rush of dizziness at the implications of her words. Feeling a little sick, he asked, "So what now?"

She pointed to the stairway. "Down there. Follow the steps to the bottom, and then go along the passageway. Remember to use the bough I gave you. It will help you speak to Arthur, too."

"Oh great," he said sarcastically. "I seem to spend my time in dark underground tunnels. I suppose it would be too much to expect his tomb to be somewhere light and pleasant. And how do I find my way in the dark?" He had visions of his torch battery failing and leaving him in the blackness.

She leaned forward and pulled a flaming branch from the fire, muttering a few words over it. She handed it to Tom wordlessly.

Tom grabbed the torch and headed towards the steps, wondering why he'd allowed himself to become involved.

As he started down the steps she shouted, "Do not turn off the main path!"

Tom had been descending for hours, slithering on the steps that widened and narrowed, switching between earth and stone, sometimes crumbling beneath his feet. The torch spluttered and flared as he encountered unexpected breezes carrying damp rotten smells. Crumbling side passages led off into blackness. The air grew stale, and several times he considered turning back, before realising he might not get off the island if he didn't fulfil this quest. His limbs ached and he was hungry and thirsty. He sat down occasionally to rest his legs and drink some water, but the steps were so uncomfortable that he didn't stop for long.

Eventually he came to a wider space – a break in the stairs where he could wedge his light upright and rest properly. He was so tired he could barely think, so although this was probably the worst place in which he would ever attempt to sleep, he decided he had to get some rest. The silence that settled around him was unnerving, but he convinced himself he was safe. He rolled his pack under his head, trying to get comfortable, wondering as he settled down what the others were doing, out there in the sunlight. And what of Finnlugh? Would he come?

12 The Lakeside

For a few minutes Beansprout stood watching as Tom disappeared behind the mist, heading to some distant place she would never know.

A chill swept through her. The boat was clearly ancient; it reminded her of images she had seen of similar boats from the past. Its familiarity scared her – it was as if the past had crossed an invisible barrier and was suddenly right next to her. It challenged everything she had ever known.

Trying to shake off the feeling, and realising there was nothing she could do now to help Tom, she hurried across to where the others stood, still motionless. She stopped in front of her grandfather. His eyes were filled with tears and he gazed beyond her into the distance. She hesitated, wondering if it would be dangerous to disturb him and the others, but decided she couldn't just leave them standing there.

She reached out her hand and laid it gently on his arm. "Granddad, wake up." He remained motionless, so she shook him, watching his eyes carefully. "Granddad, can you hear me? It's me, Beansprout." She thought she detected a flicker of movement in his eyes, but then it was gone.

She sighed and moved to Woodsmoke. He was much taller than her, so she couldn't see his eyes properly. Feeling self-conscious, she touched his sleeve and then his hand, shaking it. "Woodsmoke, wake up."

He didn't stir and she sighed again. With her back to the wide expanse of grey water, she looked at the desolate moor, the windswept grass, the trees, knotted and bent, and the tall standing stones, mysterious and indifferent to her needs. She felt overwhelmingly lonely.

She panicked. "Woodsmoke, I'm scared. Don't leave me here alone!" She shook him more aggressively, and felt a pressure on her hand as he squeezed back. He shook his head as if emerging from a deep sleep, blinked a few times, and then looked down at her. She suddenly became aware that she was still holding his hand, and released it quickly, asking, "Are you OK?"

"I think so. I had the weirdest dream." He looked around. "What's going on? Where's Tom?"

"Gone. With her. And you've been bewitched. All of you." She nodded at the others. "I couldn't wake Granddad."

"And what are we supposed to do?" He moved in front of Jack, Fahey and Brenna, looking at their patient faces.

"We have to wait. Shall we try and wake them? And then we can set up camp."

Brenna and Jack roused more quickly than Fahey, who seemed to be in the deepest sleep. Smiles played across his dreaming face, and it was with the greatest reluctance that he finally woke up, annoyed to leave a perfectly good dream.

It seemed wrong to set up camp within the standing stones, so they found a spot to the side of them, behind the narrow beach. They rigged up a waterproof shelter and built a fire of dry brushwood collected from along the shore. It was mid-afternoon by the time they had finished, and they sat around the fire, warming their hands and drinking a strange herbal tea that Beansprout didn't really like, but had managed to get used to.

They talked about what they had seen while they were bewitched. Each had had a different kind of dream. Brenna's seemed to be the worst; she had dreamt her wings had been clipped and her powers of flight taken. On waking she'd been pale and panic-stricken, and had turned into a bird, flying in wide arcs across the moor. Now she sat shrugging her shoulders, as if she could feel her wings, even though they weren't there. Beansprout wondered if she was always aware of them, as if they had a presence on her human form.

Fahey described visions of the old tales that he told, rolling like a film before his closed eyes, while Jack had floated over the Realm of Earth, which was full of sights he now wanted to see. Woodsmoke had hunted deep within the old forest, chasing spectres and wolves in rich green twilight.

Retelling their magical visions made them uneasy, and they shivered, drawing closer to the fire.

"So how long do you think this will take?" Beansprout asked.

Fahey still seemed caught in the tendrils of his dreamlike trance, gazing out at the mist as if hoping to penetrate its secrets. He murmured, "It could take weeks. We have no idea of what he has to do or where he must go. I wish I was with him."

Woodsmoke frowned. "Or it could take just hours. He might be back here before nightfall."

Brenna shrugged. "I'm sure it will take longer than one night, Woodsmoke. We may as well make ourselves comfortable." She stood up and rolled her shoulders. "I'm going to see what else is happening out there." She nodded across the moor. "I'll see you later." In a blink she had gone, soaring upwards until she was only a black speck.

Beansprout was fascinated by the standing stones. She walked around them, her fingers tracing the carvings, feeling the warmth of the stone against her palm. How long had they stood here, unchanged by the wind, rain and burning sun? Who had made them? It must have taken a long time to carve these beautiful shapes and figures, with their detailed expressions of fear, wonder and horror. She recognised some of the creatures from the carvings they had seen on the gateways, and in the great cavern in the Realm of Water, but others were strange and unnerving – creatures with tentacles, multiple limbs, large eyes, pointed teeth, snarling expressions and sharp claws. She should have felt frightened, but instead felt wonder at being in such a place; that such a place could exist. Beansprout felt suspended at the edge of the world, hovering between the known of her past and the unknown of her future. She had moved from one set of expectations to another, and should have been scared at this uncertainty, but felt only excitement.

She looked over to where her grandfather stood talking to Fahey, gestures filling the space between them, and understood why he would want to stay here. The limits of his life had shifted dramatically. His best friend was a bard, a dreamer and spinner of magic. His words conjured worlds and images, desires and hopes; they chased away the old normal, replacing it with breath-taking strangeness and wonder. In fact, this whole place was a breath-taking wonder.

Beansprout realised she didn't care how long they had

to wait. It didn't seem to matter anymore. The important thing was being here, to witness whatever happened. She wondered if this was the spell the Lady of the Lake had cast upon her, but then admitted to herself that this feeling had been growing for some time, it had just taken until now to recognise it.

She had been here only a matter of days, but already it felt like a lifetime. She had no idea what was happening at home, and wasn't sure that she really cared. Hopefully no one was frantic with worry – perhaps their absence hadn't been noticed; maybe some mysterious magic had taken care of that. She nodded to herself. Yes, that would be for the best.

Brenna loved flying. The currents were like silk against her skin, and she felt her feathers ruffling and settling as she adjusted her flight. She angled herself so that she coasted comfortably on cushions of air, and for a while just enjoyed being. She watched the others far below, curious as to the turn of events that had brought them here, with two humans she barely knew. She hoped Tom and Beansprout could help, but wondered how that was possible – they knew nothing of this place, and had no powers.

A sudden faraway movement on the edge of her vision caught her attention, and she stopped her musing and turned. She could see a patch of darkness on the land. She dropped, searching for other currents and headed towards it.

Woodsmoke lay on his back and gazed at Brenna flying high above him, a small speck against the blue. He felt lazy, glad to rest after days of travel. The sun was setting and the horizon was edged with an orange glow. The silence here was deep and endless, and it lulled his senses.

Just as he was drifting to sleep, his attention snapped to Brenna, plunging quickly earthwards. Catching another air current she soared away to his left, heading to where the edge of the moor hit the woods. He rolled on his side and, propped on his arms, gazed after her, wondering what had caught her attention. Feeling uneasy, he jumped to his feet and checked the saddlebags for his weapons. If there was an attack, they were horribly exposed. There was nowhere to shelter, and nowhere to run.

Brenna wheeled on the air currents, landing softly next to the beach where the others were gathered around the fire. The dusk was thickening, the grass turning inky blue in the hollows across the moor. The flames flickered and the wood spat, the only sound on the otherwise silent moor.

"Others are coming." She looked at Woodsmoke with concern.

"What others?"

"The Royal Houses seem to have left their under-palaces. Prince Finnlugh leads them, and I saw the Duchess of Cloy. There were about twenty guards with them."

"Damn! What does he want? This can only mean trouble."

"Not necessarily," said Fahey, "they may be here to help. Historically they're not fans of the Queen."

"I don't trust them, but there's really not much we can do against so many of them, is there?" He turned to Brenna. "How long until they're here?"

"They are far away, on the edge of the moor, but even so they travel much quicker than we do. Maybe two days?"

"That gives us a little time. Well, I don't think Tom will be back tonight. Let's get some sleep. We need to be ready for whatever happens. I'll take first watch, and I'll wake you in a few hours." Brenna nodded in agreement.

Prince Finnlugh, Bringer of Starfall and Chaos, sat on his horse and waited impatiently for the rest of the group to catch up. His horse fretted beneath him, as anxious as he was to continue. He had reached the edge of the woodlands, and the moor stretched out in front of him. He was annoyed. It had taken too long to persuade the others to act.

After Tom and Beansprout had freed him, he had strode about his palace unleashing his fury on the unsuspecting wood sprites who lounged around, drunk on his wine and beer, fattened by his food and lazy with arrogance. He had blasted them into various parts of the known and unknown universe. The lucky ones were dead; the others would be left to an uncertain fate in whatever place they ended up in.

The fight with his brother had been unsatisfactory. He had tried to shrivel him to the size of a walnut, sending a spell that would suck every inch of moisture out of him. But his brother was wily and clever, and the Prince narrowly avoided being splintered into a million pieces by a well-aimed curse. The Duke had managed to escape, leaving behind him a trail of destruction and a large hole in the rounded walls of his palace. The Prince had no doubt he had fled to Aeriken Forest, to recover. But the worst news was that he had escaped with the Starlight Jewel. The Prince had to get it back before the Duke learnt to master it.

He had sealed the palace, creating new spells to protect it, and then went to work waking the members of the

Royal Houses strewn across his ballroom floor. His brother's attack had been perfectly timed. The other members of the under-palaces had been visiting for a ball, so not only was his own household there, but all of the others too.

His brother had put a strong sleeping spell on them that took some time to break, and when they did wake they were groggy and confused. Old Prince Featherfoot would probably never be the same again. As outraged as they were by the attack, they hadn't wanted to retaliate, preferring to hole up in their palaces as they had done for centuries, trying to avoid trouble. It was the Duchess of Cloy who finally saw sense.

"My dear Cloy," the Prince had sneered. "If it has happened here, it could happen to you! Do you think this will just go away? That they will not attack again? This is not over."

"I shall seal my Palace of Scents so that no one will ever get in again," she had raged. "Do you think I'm weak?"

"I am the strongest of all of us, and I was still attacked."

"You were betrayed by your greedy infantile brother. No one will betray me."

"We are weaker if we remain isolated and alone, my dear stupid Madame!" he had said, raising an arched eyebrow. "Don't you think he covets your treacherous scents that beguile and bewitch? He may already have raided your palace. He might well be selling your secrets right now! Now we know he is not to be trusted, he is free to act openly. And he won't stop there. We don't know what he will do! I have no idea what he will do! No one will be safe unless we capture him."

He knew she couldn't bear to think of her secrets

escaping. Her creamy skin was flushed with rose, and her ruby red hair, which looked like flower petals, quivered in a mound high on her head. Rich earthy scents with a hint of sulphur rose from her skin as her rage increased. "He wouldn't dare."

"There is no one to stop him, apart from us. Unless we count the Queen; she is the only one as powerful as me. However, it seems she has made some sort of alliance with him, and is on his side. I fear she wants the Starlight Jewel."

Now he had her attention.

"And how do you suggest we stop them?" she asked icily.

"With help. And I think I know where we can get it."

Eventually she agreed to accompany him, along with a small company of the Royal Guard. The rest returned to the under-palaces to protect them, and Prince Ironroot was placed in charge. And now they were heading to the lake. If Tom was waking the King, he wanted to be there.

13 Arthur's Icy Tomb

Tom awoke with a start. The torch was still burning strongly and he had no idea what time it was. He stretched, drank some water and ate some dry biscuits. He was so hungry his stomach growled. Other than the flickering torchlight, he was surrounded by a musty blackness. The path ahead was shrouded in darkness, and his pool of light billowed from small draughts. Heaviness settled on him; the weighty expectation of his strange inheritance. He pulled his sleeve up to look at his birthmark.

It seemed to move in the torchlight, and he ran his fingers over it as if he might feel its edges raised and different from his normal skin. But it felt the same as usual. He hadn't really taken notice of it before, and to him its darker tone didn't even look like a sword.

Suddenly fearful of remaining where he was a second longer, he gathered his things and started down the path.

He could hear voices – whisperings and murmurs. He came across a tiny warm yellow light in a passage off to his right, the entrance marked by a metal gate on rusty hinges. As he paused before it, the gate swung wide in welcome. The yellow light flared brightly at the end of the passage, and scented air raced out to envelop him. It looked so welcoming and warm, and he was so cold that he decided to investigate. He stepped closer and the light flared even brighter, but as he laid his hand on the gate his own torch flickered and nearly went out, causing him to halt sharply. He stepped back warily as Vivian's warning came to him – stay on the path. A shriek pierced the silence and the light at the end of the passage flared white and then disappeared. As the breeze carried the smell of rotten flesh towards him, and the shriek faded away, Tom fled. He felt sick with fear. Taking some deep breaths he noticed the torchlight was once again burning strong and bright. He wouldn't forget Vivian's instructions a second time.

As Tom plunged deeper underground it became colder and colder, until by the time he reached the bottom of the steps his breath appeared as icy clouds. There was now only one route to follow – a passageway thick with frost that disappeared into intense darkness. Feeling he was nearing his goal, he set off quickly, his torchlight reflecting on the walls as a dull spark of orange. He began to imagine he could see things emerging out of the blackness, and then thought he heard something pattering behind him. Instead of slowing to listen, he started to walk even quicker until he was almost jogging. Then he had a horrible thought, that he might plunge into a hole in the floor or miss a turning, so he slowed down again. His hands and nose were freezing and he started to shiver.

Finally he saw dim light ahead, and emerged into a long cavern. Murky green light was filtering through a low transparent roof, and a flash of movement overhead made him realise he was under the lake. There were fish and … other things. Things that seemed very big.

It was like being in an aquarium. But he couldn't work out what the roof was made of. Maybe crystal or thickened glass. Or ice. The floor was made of huge flat slabs of stone, and in the centre was a rectangular tomb made of thick ice.

Deep within it he could see the shadowy shape of a man.

Tom sighed with relief. He'd made it. Now he just needed to work out what to do. If Arthur wasn't dead, why was he in a tomb?

He tried to push the lid off, but it was heavy and sealed shut.

The cavern walls were covered in thick frozen vines. Some had spread across the roof, and a small tangle of vines had grown across the tomb. He remembered the silver branch. Did he need to use it here?

He pulled it from his backpack, his cold fingers fumbling. Its silvery brightness glowed in the dim green light. He walked around the cavern peering at the vines, hoping the branch in his hand would fit somewhere. Nothing.

He plonked his backpack on the ground and sat beside the tomb, staring at the sleeping man below the ice. Something glinted in the figure's hands, something which ran the length of his body. Excalibur. Made by faeries as a gift for Merlin. How weird was this? He put the silver branch down on the tomb and pulled the water from his pack. There was hardly any left, and he might need to share it, assuming he could somehow wake the King. They would have to climb all the way out again. What if the King was old and decrepit? Or weak from sleeping for hundreds of years?

Contact with the tomb seemed to be doing something to the silver branch. Its brightness was decreasing – it was turning back into wood, as it had been when Vivian gave it to him. Now shoots were sprouting rapidly, and tendrils spread across the tomb. As they touched the old frozen vines, these started thawing and growing too.

Tom leapt backwards, away from the tomb as the

vines spread and the walls started moving with green wriggling growth. The tomb was soon invisible under a mass of vines, and the bough returned to silver, glinting under the fresh growth. How on earth was he supposed to get into the tomb now?

He glanced back towards the entrance and saw with a shock that it was completely smothered in vines, and with a rumble the weight of them pulled the earth down. He was trapped.

Thick shoots were now punching their way through the tomb's weakening ice. The cavern walls began to drip with moisture as the temperature warmed. Chunks of the icy tomb fell to the floor, and puddles formed beneath his feet. Tom pocketed the silver bough, put his backpack on, and began to pull chunks of ice away in an effort to speed things up.

A movement in the wall opposite stopped him momentarily. He felt a breeze and heard a dull roar. What now? He stood looking warily at the wall and felt a splash of cold water on his head. Then he saw drops hitting the floor across the cavern. He looked up with horror. The roof was melting. He would drown if he didn't get out of here quickly.

Tom grabbed the torch, ran to the wall and pushed aside the vines. Thrusting the torch forward he saw another long passageway, and he could hear running water.

Something slid and crashed behind him, and he heard a groan. His heart in his mouth, he span round and saw Arthur roll free of the ice. The King rose onto his hands and knees, breathing deeply, and then stood slowly, as if it were a great effort. Excalibur lay at his feet.

He was younger than Tom had expected, and tall with a powerful build. For a few seconds he looked dazed, then he focused on Tom, saying something that Tom couldn't understand.

Tom shook his head. "What? I'm sorry, I can't understand you. Look, we're under the lake and we have to go. Now!" Tom grabbed Arthur by the arm and pulled him towards the vines.

Arthur resisted, again saying something Tom couldn't understand.

Tom pointed upwards at the dripping roof, trying to show the urgency of their situation. "We have to go – now!" He pulled on Arthur's arm again.

Arthur looked up and around the cavern, and then understanding dawned. He sheathed his sword and staggered after Tom, who pushed through the vines and set off quickly along the tunnel.

Every few metres Tom glanced behind him, but Arthur kept up. The passageway led to an underground river running alongside the path. The floor was slick beneath them, glinting in the flickering light, and the roar of water became louder as they began to climb upwards. Then, abruptly, they reached a steep crumbling rock face. To their right, a waterfall tumbled over the rocks, spray filling the air around them.

Tom peered upwards into the darkness, and wondered how high they would have to climb. He gripped the torch tightly. If he dropped it they would be in total blackness. With his other hand he sought hand-holds as he clambered up the treacherous path. Arthur slipped and muttered behind him.

Tom had the horrible feeling the entire journey back to the surface was going to be this difficult. He wanted the stairs back. If the cavern roof cracked it would flood, as would the path they were on. He did not want to drown. Don't think of anything, he thought, but climbing and keep climbing. Hand over hand, upwards and upwards. His limbs burned and his fingers were sore and bruised. His chest ached with every breath he took. Beyond his laboured breathing and the roar of the waterfall, he heard and felt a deeper rumble. Was that the roof collapsing?

Just when he thought he couldn't climb any longer, the path started to level out and the roof came into view not far above his head. He collapsed onto the ground, gasping for breath, closely followed by Arthur who lay next to him, chest heaving.

Tom wondered why Arthur couldn't understand him; this would make life tricky. And then it struck him – Vivian had said to use the branch. He pulled it out of his pocket and, nudging Arthur with his foot, handed it to him. Arthur sat up, looking puzzled. "Why are you giving me this?"

"Yes! I can understand you! It worked."

Arthur looked shocked and then smiled. "What an interesting trick!" He turned the bough over and over in his hands, as if it would reveal its secrets, then handed it back to Tom, looking at him intently. "To whom do I owe my life?"

"My name is Tom, and I was sent by Vivian to wake you. I didn't really plan on it, you know." And because he was still feeling annoyed, he added, "It wasn't my choice. I had to do it. And I'm not very happy about it."

"Well, Tom, my reluctant rescuer, I am Arthur, and I'm not sure I'm very happy about it either."

"I do know who I'm rescuing!"

Arthur laughed and gazed beyond Tom. "Well, Tom, I can see a boat, so let us use that, because I don't think I can walk much further. I find I am weak, but hope I will regain my strength soon."

Tom saw Arthur was right. They were on the edge of water – not a river, something bigger. He could feel a change in the air and in the sounds around them. The far side was hidden in blackness, but there was a small boat pulled up onto the shore. On his right the water churned and raced before pouring over the edge.

They pushed the boat into the water and clambered in, bobbing unevenly as they sat on narrow benches. Tom propped the torch in the prow as they looked for ways to move the boat, but within seconds the boat started to move on its own.

Arthur murmured, "The Lady of the Lake is always resourceful."

Tom just grunted in reply. There were other things he'd have said about her.

"And where are we, Tom? Other than underground."

"Well, we're not in England any more. We are in The Other, The Land of the Fey, or something of the sort."

Arthur nodded slowly. "Ah! Merlin's deal. I didn't really believe that. I should have known better."

The boat moved silently across the inky blackness of the lake, the roof low and uneven over their heads. They had come such a long way that Tom guessed they were travelling back to the lakeshore, not the Isle of Avalon. He glanced up, unsettled that there was water above them and below, with the possibility of more water arriving. If the cavern flooded, the water level would start to rise, and there wasn't much room for that.

Arthur lay down, eyes closed, his head on the edge of the boat, his feet under the bench. Tom guessed he was in his thirties. His hair was long and dark, and he had a short beard. His sword lay sheathed at his side, and the hilt's strange engravings flashed in the light. Had he only been this old when he'd died? Or had he been put into a magical sleep? Or had faerie magic made him younger?

Tom looked again at his birthmark, comparing it with the sword next to Arthur. Was it his imagination or did his birthmark look sharper than before, like the real Excalibur? Were there shapes coiling in the centre? Shaking his head as if to free himself from a trance, he covered his arm and shivered.

Without warning they plunged into mist. Mist underground? Faerie magic again. Tom was exhausted. He lay down in the bottom of the boat and gazed at the roof passing overhead, trusting that Vivian would protect them.

14 Waiting and Watching

The group at the lakeside slept later than usual, but it was still earlier than Beansprout would ever rise at home. The first thing she did after waking was feel her arm, where the spear had punctured it. It was healing quickly now, and it had begun to itch. It would leave a scar. She smiled; she had a battle wound.

As she rolled on to her back she saw the blue sky above her, pale like a duck egg. She sat up, clutching the blanket around her shoulders, and faced the wall of mist stretched across the lake. Her grandfather and Fahey were still dozing, but someone had added wood to the fire and it blazed brightly. A kettle hung above it, steam seeping from its spout.

She smiled with contentment. She could get used to this. It felt so freeing to be lying on the lakeshore beside a fire. She felt she could do anything, go anywhere. Anything she needed she had with her.

Before they'd gone to sleep last night, Fahey had insisted on telling one of his tales – to help them relax, he'd said. He told a tale about an ancient king who outwitted a forest goblin. It was very funny, particularly as he paced around the fire acting out the parts. Beansprout presumed he was trying to make them feel brave, and it sort of worked.

She grabbed her dirty cup from beside her and walked over to the lake to swill it, before refilling it with sweet herb tea. Sitting down again she looked around for Brenna and Woodsmoke. She presumed Brenna was flying, but where was Woodsmoke? She swivelled to look back over the moor. Grasses and heathers rippled all the way to the horizon, a blackish-green line where the wood began. To the north was the old forest – Aeriken Forest. She rolled it around her tongue, and tried to imagine what mysteries it contained. Woodsmoke had told her it was the home and hunting grounds of the Aerikeen, and that some of the Realm of the Earth's stranger creatures lived there.

She looked for signs that Prince Finnlugh was approaching, but saw only unbroken grass and scrub. A figure bobbed over to the left. Woodsmoke, emerging from one of the hollows.

"I think we should move," he said as he sat down next to her. "The hollow over there is broad and deep, sheltered from the wind, and more importantly will give us cover from unwelcome attention."

"Do you really think we're in danger?"

"I don't know, but I'd rather we at least try and hide."

"Wouldn't we be better heading back to the Tor? At least we'd be high, and able to defend ourselves."

"It would take too long. And what if Tom arrives back here and finds himself alone, without help?"

"He'd better not be on his own!"

"Even if he's with the King, we can't leave him here."

"No, I know. It was just a suggestion. What if they surround us – around the hollow?"

"They're more likely to head for the shore, then we can retreat back across the moor."

"Without Tom?"

"He might be here by then. Stop being awkward."

"Sorry." She looked sheepish. "Just trying to help. OK, let's pack up and hide in the hollow."

"If you two have finished bickering, I would like to agree," said Jack, stirring from his blankets. "Let's head for the hollow. I feel a bit exposed here."

Brenna returned at midday. She had ranged over the moor and woods, but not over the thick canopy of Aeriken.

"The Prince and his company are nearly halfway across the moor," she said.

Beansprout gasped. "But they move so quickly. It took us days to travel that far."

"They have a far greater magic than we ever will," said Woodsmoke, "and their horses are swifter and more powerful. They're bred from an ancient line of magical beasts."

"It is said that one of the royal line came with his followers to the lakeshore, millennia ago, to raise a new house," said Fahey. "He wanted to solve the mystery of the lake and reach the Isle of Avalon. But not even he was strong enough to do that." He sighed regretfully.

"Why, what happened to him?"

"He disappeared and was never seen again. His cries echoed through the halls day and night, and many perished trying to find him. They abandoned the place in the end. No one could stand it there."

"Where was it?"

He nodded downwards. "Somewhere beneath our feet!"

Beansprout looked uncomfortably at the ground below them.

"I'm going to remain out there, as a bird," said

Brenna, "perched on the standing stones. I can keep watch for them – and for Tom." She flitted out of the hollow.

"I've changed my mind" grumbled Fahey. "I don't like hiding here, it makes me feel like a coward. And I can't see what's going on."

Woodsmoke gave him a long impatient look, filled with distaste. "We are not hiding like cowards, we are trying to protect ourselves from attack, old man. Are you going to produce a sword from under that cloak?"

"That's unfair and you know it."

"Apart from your skill with words, have you anything that could protect us?"

"I might know a few charms that could make us invisible, a protection from unwanted eyes." He looked sly, as if he was doing things he shouldn't.

"Good, do it."

The light was falling and long shadows were stretching over the ground when Brenna returned. They sat at the base of the hollow, a bright fire burning merrily, eating a supper of stewed rabbit that filled the air with a rich warm smell.

Beansprout was relieved they had moved camp. It was so much warmer out of the moorland wind, and it felt safer somehow.

Woodsmoke sighed. "I don't think Tom will appear tonight. I had hoped we'd be out of here before Finnlugh arrived, but now …"

Beansprout adjusted the blanket across her shoulders and, turning to Fahey, said, "Maybe to pass the time you should tell us another tale."

"I have many. Any particular one?"

"Yes. I would like to know more about Arthur."

"There are many such tales. Arthur's knights, Arthur's battles, Arthur and Merlin …"

"I'd just like to know a little bit about him."

"Then I shall keep it simple. Centuries ago, Britain was in turmoil. There were many kings, fighting for power and land, and then outsiders came who fought them all. One king, Uther, was more powerful than most, and he had a very clever man as his advisor. He was called Merlin.

"There were rumours that Merlin was a wizard. They said he could control the elements – earth, water, air and fire; that he could turn night to day, control animals and cross to the Otherworld. At that time the paths between both worlds were easier to walk, if you knew where to look. Many fey and humans passed to and fro, and Merlin crossed many times.

"Uther had a son, called Arthur. He was born in Tintagel, Uther's castle by the sea. Merlin spent much time with him, teaching him many things. The things he couldn't teach, he made sure Arthur learnt from other skilled men.

"Uther's son grew strong, and yet he was a gentle man, keen to talk with his enemies rather than fight. But when he did fight, everyone marvelled at his strong hands and quick feet. Warriors admired his skill and pledged him allegiance.

"When Uther died, Arthur became king, but the time was fraught with danger. In spite of the invading outsiders the kings still fought each other ferociously. Merlin wanted to give Arthur a weapon with magical powers to protect him in battle, and which would unite the people. He crossed through the mists to the Otherworld to bargain for such a weapon.

"His friend Vivian had magical powers, and great influence amongst the fey. She was wise and gentle and lived upon the Isle of Avalon that straddled both worlds. She spoke to the Forger of Light, who agreed to make a sword – Excalibur. But in exchange for this magical weapon, Arthur had to come to the Otherworld when his life was all but over, to rest until he was needed. Merlin felt he had little choice and agreed to the bargain, though he never forgave Vivian for it.

"So Merlin performed one of his greatest feats of magic. In order to prove the sword's powers, and Arthur's power to rule over all, he set the sword in a great stone, telling the kings that whoever could withdraw the sword would be the one and only true King of Britain. Many tried and many failed, all except Arthur. He withdrew the sword from the stone as if he were pulling it from butter. And he held it aloft, and the sun struck it and dazzled those watching, and they fell at his feet acknowledging he was the one true King.

"These warriors became his knights, and to promote fairness and equality Arthur had them sit at a round table, and the land of Britain united to fight and repel the newcomers. His court was at Camelot and it dazzled beneath the sun and moon like a shining jewel. Arthur ruled for years and years. His knights fought, quested, feasted and held tournaments; his people loved him and the land was at peace.

"But in the land of light, some still sought the shadows.

"Arthur had an older half-sister, called Morgan le Fay. She resented the time that Merlin gave to Arthur, and she begrudged Arthur's success. Morgan was half-fey and half-human, and a powerful sorceress. Merlin didn't trust her. She conspired against Arthur, seeking to destroy him. Using her magic arts, she lured Arthur's nephew, Mordred, with promises of power and wealth. She filled his head with lies and trained him to kill Arthur. She was patient, waiting and watching until Arthur was distracted. And finally the time came.

"Arthur was betrayed by his wife, Guinevere. She was beautiful but weak, and desired Sir Lancelot, one of Arthur's greatest knights. And Lancelot desired her. When Arthur found out, Guinevere was banished and Lancelot fled the kingdom, swiftly pursued by Arthur who chased Lancelot far and wide, full of anger and vengeance.

"Morgan seized her chance. By the time Arthur returned, Mordred had taken the land. They fought in the great Battle of Camlann, and Arthur was mortally wounded. As required by the bargain, Arthur's body was carried to the lakeshore from whence he could be taken to Avalon. Excalibur was thrown into the lake as a signal to Vivian, and she emerged from the mists with her eight sister priestesses to escort Arthur to the Other.

"And Britain fell into darkness."

That night, Beansprout dreamt of Vivian and the large bronze boat with the dragon-headed prow coming to take Arthur to Avalon, in the same way as Vivian had taken Tom to wake the King.

15 Strange Alliances

Tom sensed that the lake had narrowed – something in the air seemed to have changed. He daydreamed as the unreality of his situation nagged at his brain, lying on his back and gazing up at the thick tendrils of mist obscuring his view.

Again he had the feeling of not moving, of being suspended in time and place, caught forever in a pocket of air between two lakes.

Arthur was motionless beside him. Tom couldn't understand how a man who had slept for hundreds of years could want to sleep again. Feeling charitable, he put it down to physical exhaustion. It had been an abrupt awakening. Finding yourself on the floor of an underground cavern after being asleep, in ice, for hundreds of years, would be very odd. He wondered if Arthur could remember dying? He would ask him when he woke up.

He wanted to sit up and look around, but the mist continued to hide the low roof and he didn't want to hit his head, so he remained lying down. He was bored, and felt as if he had been in the dark forever.

Tom lost track of time. He heard a strange distant shout and thought his ears were playing tricks, but then he heard it again, coming closer. His skin prickled with goosebumps and he froze. Something was coming towards them. Again, a moan and a splash. He rolled onto his stomach and peered over the edge of the boat, dreading that he might see something there, but all was darkness except for the small sphere of torchlight on mist and water. He hurriedly lay down again and the sound stopped. He wanted to see the sky again and feel a warm breeze. When he got out of here, it was time to go home.

Eventually a soft grey light banished the darkness and the mist disappeared, revealing a high, vaulted natural roof. Tom sat up and peered into the gloom. They were again on a river, but to their right was a large, seemingly unending cavern, like an underground cathedral. Huge columns reached up to a carved stone roof.

Tom nudged Arthur. "Wake up, look at this."

Arthur barely stirred, but Tom kept prodding him with his foot, unable to take his eyes from the cavern. He wanted to get out of the boat. They must be near the lakeshore now.

As if the boat had read his thoughts, it steered to the riverbank and stopped.

Arthur sat up, bleary-eyed. He looked as amazed as Tom. "Where are we?"

"I've no idea, but I think we might find a way out."

They clambered out onto shallow stone steps and entered the silent halls that glowed with pale light. Their footsteps echoed as they walked past soaring columns, stairways that crumbled halfway up walls, and doorways that stood empty and dark. There was no obvious source of the light, except perhaps from the stone itself.

Arthur carried his sword in readiness, although there were no signs of life. Tom carried the torch – just in case darkness fell once more. He thought this was possibly the weirdest place he'd been so far. It was creepy because it was so obviously deserted. But someone had lived here, someone had built this. Who?

A long wailing cry echoed in the air, and Tom halted in alarm. "What the hell was that?"

They turned quickly, looking in all directions, but the hall was empty.

"I heard that earlier, on the lake," said Tom. "This place is freaky. Let's find an exit, quickly!"

Another wail punctuated the silence.

"Tom."

"Yes," he answered impatiently.

"Look down."

Tom did so, and saw water lapping gently across the floor.

"The cave roof must have collapsed. The cavern's flooding."

"Vivian doesn't like to make life too easy, does she?" Arthur muttered angrily.

They ran along corridors and sloshed through rooms while the water continued to rise, until eventually they came to a broad set of stone stairs ascending to another level.

"This will buy us some time," Tom said, relieved.

On the next level they saw rooms stretching away on either side, but the stairs continued to climb. Carrying on upwards, they came to a sealed circular space.

"There are no doors here," Arthur said.

"There has to be some way out," Tom said. "Start looking."

They examined the walls closely, feeling along the cracks, hoping to find a hidden opening or some sort of mechanism, but with no success.

"Let's try the floor, Tom," said Arthur. "Look, there's an interesting pattern right in the middle, and maybe …" He broke off as he pressed a small depression in one of the centre stones.

With a rumble and a grating sound that set Tom's teeth on edge, stones started to shoot up around them.

Arthur looked at him and grinned. "Exactly as I thought."

The floor formed itself into a series of steps that joined up with steps descending from above. Blue sky winked through an opening in the roof, and Tom sighed with relief. Neither of them could get up the stairs fast enough.

They emerged in the centre of the standing stones. The sun was dropping towards the horizon and the stones' shadows fell long and dark across the moor.

Brenna stood at the edge of the circle, grinning broadly, while Woodsmoke, Beansprout, Fahey and Jack raced over the moor, almost colliding with Brenna. Woodsmoke looked relieved and Beansprout rushed over to hug Tom, but Fahey, although pleased, looked far more interested in the gaping hole beneath them.

"Tom, you're back! You did it!" whooped Jack, grabbing Tom in a bear hug.

Tom grinned broadly at them. "I guess I did. Let me introduce you to Arthur."

Arthur stepped forward, greeting them each in turn. Beansprout blushed as Arthur took her hand and kissed it. The myth had become a man.

As they stood shaking hands, Tom glanced beyond them puzzled, "Who's that?"

They all turned and groaned, except for Beansprout, who was extremely curious to meet the much talked of and mysterious Royal Houses. The setting sun fell on the

approaching Prince and his group; their silver armour
flashed, the horses' black coats gleamed, and their pennants
fluttered in the wind as they raced across the moor towards
them.

"Prince Finnlugh, Bringer of Starfall and Chaos, and a
few friends …" Brenna explained, her eyebrows raised and a
smile playing across her lips.

"He came?" Tom asked.

"So much for trying to hide," Woodsmoke groaned.

Fahey looked at the hole, then at Tom. "So where did
you come from, Tom?"

"You won't believe what's down there," he said.

"I bet I will," said Fahey, smirking.

Woodsmoke ignored them all and walked to the edge
of the standing stones, Brenna at his side, watching the
approaching riders. The Prince and his party drew closer in a
swirl of wind and thundering hooves. Coming to a stop, the
Prince jumped down and strode quickly towards Tom and
Arthur. Before he could get close, however, Woodsmoke
stopped him, stepping directly into his path.

"What do you want here, Prince Finnlugh?"

"I was invited," he replied, looking past Woodsmoke
towards Brenna and Tom, his eyes finally coming to rest on
Arthur. "I wanted to know if it was true." He looked at
Woodsmoke. "I'm not here to cause trouble."

"Then you are welcome," said Brenna, and she led the
way to the others.

It was a strange company that gathered that night on the
edge of the moor, the brooding wall of mist on the lake
marking the edge of the visible world. Several camp fires had
been lit, and the Prince and the Duchess had magically

erected enormous pavilions for shelter, grown from the heathers and small bushes that lay thickly around them.

Before darkness had fallen, Fahey and several of the Prince's party had been unable to resist descending the great stone steps leading to the underground palace. Not that they could explore far – the water continued to rise and the lower floor was now completely submerged.

Tom lounged on a couch, revelling in his moment of glory. He tried to work out how deep he had been and how far he'd travelled, but time and distance had lost all meaning. He was amazed to find that only two days had passed – it felt more like a week. He looked across to where Arthur sat by the fire, surrounded by people pressing him with questions. Fahey was gazing at him gleefully, unable to get enough of this unexpected figure from the past. Tom felt he should be more awed than he actually was, but he was so exhausted from the pace of the previous days that he couldn't properly take anything in. It was too unreal.

He was more curious about the oddities of the Prince's party. The Duchess of Cloy had a towering mass of hair like an enormous wedding cake piled on her head. At least, he thought it was hair, but it looked like petals. She wore a pendant around her neck, on which hung a large green stone mounted on gold – but the stone rested at the back of her neck rather than at her throat. He was unnerved when it blinked like an eye, and even more unnerved when the Duchess turned around and gazed at him for long seconds. He could smell violets, sweet and overpowering, and then as she turned away the smell vanished, leaving him feeling giddy and sick.

They were all odder than Woodsmoke, Brenna and Fahey. He hadn't realised how much he'd grown used to his friends' otherness. But the people, or rather the fey, from the Royal Houses were very strange. Some had peach-like skin, soft and furry; others had skin as smooth as cream, or skin covered with whiskers. Their hair was like silk, or balls of cotton candy, coloured like rainbows or as white as snow. They were draped in magic; it crackled over them like static electricity.

Beansprout sat next to him. "You all right? You're very quiet."

"I'm exhausted. The rescuing business is hard work."

She laughed. Tom had related how he'd woken Arthur, and the mad dash through the tunnel and onto the underground lake.

"I think Woodsmoke is feeling happier about the Prince." They looked to where Woodsmoke and the Prince sat next to the fire, speaking earnestly. "I wonder what happens now?"

"Back home I guess," Tom said.

Beansprout took a deep breath. "I don't want to go back, Tom."

"What? Are you kidding me?"

"No. I love it here. I have room to think. I'm not going, and you can't make me."

"You can't not go home. What would your mum say? She'd freak out."

Beansprout shrugged. "It's just the way I feel."

"You might feel it now, but you won't forever. What will you do? You're being crazy. This isn't real," he said, gesturing at everything around them.

"Of course it's real. It's just a different real."

"But you don't belong here."

"But I could," she said stubbornly. Getting up, she

left him and walked back towards Woodsmoke. Sighing, and getting to his feet with difficulty, Tom followed.

The Prince was gazing at Arthur's sword. It glinted in the firelight, which illuminated the rich and fantastical engravings along its polished blade and hilt. "Merlin was a powerful man to negotiate that for you, Arthur," he said admiringly.

Arthur laughed. "Merlin liked to get his own way, and generally did. Until his luck ran out." He sighed deeply, his laughter gone, and he gazed back to the fire. "It's because of that sword that I'm here, honouring his bargain, when I should be dust by now."

"You have a purpose, Arthur."

"It seems so. The Lady has decided I must stop the Queen."

"And I must stop my brother. We can help each other."

"How?"

"Travel together, into Aeriken. I think they are working together; why shouldn't we?"

"You don't need me. I don't have powerful magic."

"Neither do I at the moment. I am weakened by the loss of my jewel. But you have Excalibur; it is a talisman, forged by faeries and full of protection. And besides, Vivian seems to think differently. She woke you especially for this reason. And I can help you!"

Woodsmoke and Brenna were watching this exchange with interest. And no wonder, thought Tom. A Prince who had isolated himself and his retinue in his under-palace for years, and an ancient King of Britain, far from home, brought back from the dead.

The Prince turned to them. "I'd like your help, too."

"How could I possibly help you?" asked Woodsmoke. "I have less magic than you, and I don't have an all-powerful sword."

"But you are a hunter and a tracker. If anyone can help find my brother, it should be you! And I bet you know Aeriken better than anyone here, except for perhaps … you my dear," he said, turning to Brenna. "You can fly, and therefore must be of the Aerikeen, ruled by our beloved murderous Queen Gavina. Therefore you can help us in other ways."

Brenna's face drained of colour and she turned away abruptly.

"Oh come now, Brenna. You must want to stop her. She's hurting your people! Here's your chance," Finnlugh said in his most persuasive tones.

16 Aeriken Forest

The trees of Aeriken Forest grew closely together, as if trying to repel newcomers. The thick green canopy was suffocating, the branches forming a tight tangled knot overhead, and the forest interior was dim and soupy.

The track was narrow, forcing the band of travellers into a strung out, winding line.

They had been in the forest for several days now, but there was still no sign of the Duke of Craven. Woodsmoke had led them to an area the sprites had lived in, but it had obviously been deserted for some time. He told them he hadn't hunted there for years, and much had changed, but said the deeper they moved into the forest, the more dangerous it would become. They would start seeing wolves and satyrs soon. Already the wolves' howls echoed through the night, sending prickles up their necks. The horses were becoming spooked, skittering nervously in the darkness, and everyone was jumpy, thinking they were seeing things in the murky gloom.

Beansprout was by now quite at home on horseback. "I think we're being watched," she said, riding beside Tom.

"Why do you think that?"

"Can't you feel it? It's like there's a million eyes on us."

"It's just this place, the Otherworld. I feel like that all the time."

"No, this forest is different. It's brooding, wondering what we're doing here."

Occasionally a figure would materialise out of a tree trunk and stand watching from a distance, barely visible, dark eyed and green skinned, before melting back into the shadows. Fahey whispered that they were dryads – spirits of the trees and guardians of the forest.

By nightfall they had changed their plan. Brenna would lead them to the Aerie, a palace built into the crags of a steep cliff deep in the forest. It seemed inevitable that the Duke would head there – if he dared risk it.

"Of course my brother will risk it. He's desperate to use the Jewel." Prince Finnlugh looked as if he was beginning to regret this march into the forest. "And we have to find him quickly, before he learns to harness its destructive powers."

"So," said Arthur, "you have brought us into the forest, but we seem to have moved no further forward. May I ask your plan? We will not succeed without one. Travelling to the palace on a whim is foolhardy."

"Good question," Woodsmoke said. "Steal back the jewel? Kill the Queen? Save her subjects and restore order to the forest?"

"I don't need sarcasm, thank you." Finnlugh turned to Arthur. "Do you have a better idea, Sir?"

"Not really." The King shook his head thoughtfully. "I feel a little unprepared. Vivian seems to think that I shall know what to do, but frankly I have no idea. I know nothing of this Queen, or what she is accused of. As you know, I have been in an enchanted sleep for a very long time. Perhaps someone can explain to me what it is she has done. Who is she?"

"She walked out of the forest and into our palace hundreds of years ago," Brenna said. "She was lost, hungry, exhausted, and needed help. I wasn't born then, but we all know the tale. She looked fragile and seemed kind, and quickly our King fell in love. His wife had died and he was lonely.

"She wasn't one of us, but he didn't care, and neither did we. They were happy, and had children and then grandchildren. But as the years went on we began to see a different side to her. She was quick-tempered, manipulative and sly. But the King couldn't see it. And then the King died and we mourned. And although his firstborn son should have become King, the Queen continued to rule.

"Slowly but surely things started to change for the worse, and when she was challenged, those who had dared to question started to disappear, particularly the heirs to the throne. And so we left, drifting away to hidden parts of Aeriken where we could not be found. Some left the forest altogether, as I did.

"And it seems she is now worse; that she has turned on even those whom she trusted."

"But how did she gain so much control?" Arthur asked.

"She tricked us with her magic, until it was too late to stop her. This had never happened to us before; we were innocent and trusting. And if we couldn't stop her then, I'm not sure we can now. She seems to have gone mad."

"Her whole court may be dead, if she has been 'hunting her own'," Woodsmoke said. "I'm just not sure what she wants with your brother, Finnlugh, or what your brother wants from her."

They were crouched around a small fire, the horses

snickering quietly, tethered to the trees. Tonight the Prince and Duchess had raised elaborate three-sided tents, protecting their backs from the cold dark eyes of the forest. Their lack of progress was beginning to annoy everyone, and the forest's atmosphere twisted their thoughts.

"And," Brenna added, "the forest has changed. There's no one here. It's as if all the forest creatures are hiding. Something is very wrong."

"I think she wants the Starlight Jewel," Finnlugh said thoughtfully. "It could greatly increase her power. Why else would the Duke be coming here?"

"Well, in that case," Arthur said quietly, "we must head to the palace."

Towering above them was the steep wall of the cliff. The top was hidden from view, shielded by clouds and mist. Despite its height, it had been impossible to see from the forest as the trees were so dense and the canopy so thick. It felt like it had taken weeks to reach it.

Mosses covered the floor, disguising fallen trees, and they stumbled along making slow progress. It didn't help that the paths to the Aerie were hidden from outsiders, and Brenna had difficulty finding them again.

The feeling of gloom had grown ever stronger, until they were barely sleeping, their dreams filled with strange images. They had taken their mind off things by sword-fighting with each other. Beansprout and Tom were given swords suitable for learning with, and Arthur taught them, saying he needed to practise too.

For the past few nights, wolves had surrounded the camp. It had taken several volleys of arrows before they'd retreated, their teeth flashing in the firelight, their eyes glinting yellow.

And then a group of dryads had appeared out of the shadows, silent and solemn, barely visible in the fire's glow. Those sitting round the fire had leapt to their feet, wondering how the dryads could have passed the guards. A dryad stepped forward asking, "What do you want here?"

Finnlugh answered, "The Queen and my brother. Nothing else."

"She will kill you. We hide from her now; everyone hides from her now. Beware your fire." And then they had vanished.

Finnlugh had put out the fire, and they had fallen silent in the dark.

At the base of the crag, they searched for hours before finding the narrow stony path to the top. They decided to leave the horses at the bottom with some of Finnlugh's Royal Guard.

There had been another argument. "You should stay here, help protect the horses," Finnlugh said to the Duchess. "I can feel very strong strange magic. Something is very wrong here."

"I did not journey all this way to look after horses," she hissed in reply.

"If and when we escape from the palace, we'll need the horses to return. And I don't want anyone following us up that hill. I have no wish to be trapped."

Jack joined in. "Actually, there's no way I can get up there without a horse. I'll stay, and so should you," he said to Tom and Beansprout.

"Not a chance," they answered at the same time.

"You have no idea how dangerous it may be!" argued Jack.

"And that's why I'm going," answered Tom. Despite weeks of moaning, he now realised he had no wish to be left out of anything.

"And don't think you'll change my mind!" Beansprout said.

Fahey looked at Jack. "I'll stay. My knees will never manage that climb, unfortunately. And they're right. They should go. I feel they're part of this."

Jack looked as if he was going to protest, but then sighed and fell silent.

"See!" Finnlugh said to the Duchess. "You need to protect them too."

She stared at him, frowning.

"You know I'm right, dear Duchess. You can feel it too."

The eye in her pendant blinked slowly, and she stroked the necklace absentmindedly, as if listening to something. "All right. But if you're not back in three days, I leave you here."

"A deal then. We start at first light."

Before they set off, the Prince and the Duchess magically built a tall fence of thick thorny wood to protect the camp. It was set back under the trees, the horses secured inside and the remaining guards positioned around the edge.

The Duchess settled herself in front of the small bright fire. Rummaging in her bags, she brought out a variety of herbs which she cast into the fire, muttering quietly. With a sizzle, the flames changed colour to smoky blues and greens, and she sat for some time in a trance, gazing into their changing shapes. Eventually she roused herself. "We shall manage without a fire again tonight."

"But the wolves – we need to keep them away!" Fahey

said.

"We must rely on the boundary. There are worse things than wolves out there. We must become invisible, we must appear dead."

"What? What's out there? And how can we appear dead?"

"We will smell dead, which will attract the wolves but keep away other things. Trust me on this, Fahey. You heard the dryads. We do not want the Queen finding us."

She moved off to prepare her magic, and Tom wondered yet again what he'd got himself into.

17 The Rotten Heart

The stony shale slid under Tom's feet and he cursed as he climbed. In places he needed to bend double against the steepness of the path. He was grumpily aware of Brenna ahead of him, stepping lightly and effortlessly.

"Brenna, why aren't you flying?" he called.

She paused and looked back at him. "I can't".

He stopped in surprise, catching his breath and stretching out his aching back. "Why not?"

"Something's stopping me."

"Like what?"

"The magic Finnlugh mentioned. It's making the air feel syrupy, so I can't fly."

"It feels fine to me," Tom replied, puzzled.

"Trust me, it's not." She turned and kept on climbing.

Tom gazed out over the forest. He'd passed clefts and hollows, and forced his way through thick vegetation. They were above the canopy now and Aeriken stretched to the horizon. His muscles burned with the effort and he was sweaty and tired. The rest of the party toiled above him, some out of view. He sighed as Brenna disappeared ahead of him, then with a great effort pushed on, muttering to himself about stupid quests.

A scream interrupted his thoughts and he looked up, pushing his hair out of his eyes. Was that Beansprout? The scream was followed by shouts and yells. Damn! He ran, cursing his aching muscles. Rounding a corner, he stumbled into Brenna and the others.

He found himself on the edge of a wide cleft reaching deep into the cliff face. At its furthest corner were the palace gates, hanging open, the entrance dark. Carved out of the rock was the Aerie. The cleft was filled with dead birds – hundreds of them. Their bodies lay thick upon the ground, bloodied, their feathers torn. The smell of decay was strong and Tom's stomach turned.

But that wasn't what had caused the shouts and screams. Spread on the cliffs above them were scores more birds, and other creatures, half-human, half-bird, their huge wings spread behind them, shackled to the rock. They were all dead. Many had rotted, leaving skeletons to bleach in the sun.

Tears poured down Brenna's face, and the rest of them stood in shock.

"Who could have done this?" said Arthur.

Nobody answered.

Arthur pulled Excalibur from its sheath. "Allow me." He pushed ahead, and the rest of them followed, peering nervously upwards. Their footsteps echoed on the rock, bounding around them. Shale slipped and slithered down, landing at Tom's feet. Woodsmoke halted briefly, his bow angled steeply upwards. Apart from wind-ruffled feathers, nothing moved. He lowered his bow and walked on.

Beyond the shattered gates of the palace was a broad hall, illuminated by beams of light slanting in from above. The roof was high overhead – if it could be called a roof.

Most of the walls were solid rock pitted with openings, out of which scrubby bushes and trees grew haphazardly, but closer to the top the walls became a lattice work of rock, open to the wind and sky. Bridges of stone arched above them, weaving backwards and forwards, higher and higher, like the spokes of a wheel.

"It's like an aviary," the Prince murmured.

"Well, we *are* birds. What did you expect?" Brenna answered abruptly. Her tears had dried and she looked pale and angry.

The floor was thick with feathers and droppings, with the odd paw print visible. "Wolves," said Woodsmoke.

Arthur scanned around. "Where to now?"

"I have no idea. I thought I'd see signs of my brother, but …" Finnlugh trailed off.

"We should go to the throne room." Brenna said. "That's where the Queen's power is concentrated. We should see what's there."

An eerie cry punctuated the air and arrows thudded into the ground around them. Some of Finnlugh's guard's were hit and fell awkwardly to the floor, arrows jutting from their bodies.

Everyone ran for shelter. Woodsmoke fired arrows above them, but their enemies were out of sight.

Brenna shouted, "This way!" and ran, zigzagging towards a dark recess in the far wall.

A body almost fell on Tom, and he stumbled as he ran round it. Next to him, Beansprout sprinted, her hair streaming behind her. The guards who had already reached the recess fired arrows back into the hall. Tom threw himself through the arch as Finnlugh shouted, "Keep behind me!" The Prince muttered something unintelligible and thrust out his hand, from which a ball of white light flew into the hall. A boom echoed off the walls, hurting their ears. Several wood sprites thudded to the floor, dead, their limbs splayed.

"My brother! He's here!" Finnlugh said. He turned with a wolfish grin. "Lead on, Madame!"

"The throne room's up there," Brenna said, pointing upwards.

"Up there?" Tom repeated, feeling his legs protesting already.

"There are steps cut into the rock on either side of the bridges," explained Brenna, "and rooms leading back into the hillside. But we have to cross the bridges to make our way up."

"I'm sure there will be more sprites up there too," Finnlugh added.

Tripping on each other's heels, they followed Brenna up the stone staircase until they reached the first bridge. Finnlugh's guards made their way quickly across, and the rest jogged after them, weapons drawn. Thankfully the way was clear, and they were able to move upwards across the first few tiered bridges, zigzagging their way across the palace.

Tom took deep breaths and tried not look down as he ran across the bridges, which were far too high and narrow for his liking. As they reached the end of each one, they paused to search for signs of life on the bridges above them and in the rooms on each level.

"Who lived here?" Beansprout asked.

"Members of the court – anyone who slept in human form rather than in bird form. It varies; depends on your mood or your duties."

"What do you mean, duties?" Arthur asked.

"The Queen demanded that most retained their human form, and we each had to serve her if we lived here. I decided to leave. It wasn't forbidden, but ..." she paused. "I made myself an outcast, and I wasn't the only one. She could be very demanding. And I had other things to fear too."

The rooms were abandoned and dirty, but there were no more bodies. "It's as if they fled and were caught outside," Brenna said.

As they stepped out onto the next bridge, another volley of arrows and spears rained down from above and they retreated quickly – except for Arthur and Tom, who were too far ahead. They ducked and dodged, managing to reach the other side unscathed. Tom had just drawn his sword when a small group of sprites thundered down the steps towards them. While Arthur leapt into action, Tom could barely think how to swing his sword and he stabbed wildly, feeling his sword sink into flesh and bone. A sprite swung at his head and, as Tom ducked, the sprite fell dead at his feet. Arthur stood behind having barely raised a sweat.

"Are you all right, Tom?"

"I'll let you know later."

Arthur and Tom ran to the top of the stairs and saw several more sprites halfway across the bridge, unaware of Tom and Arthur as they fired on the bridge below. Tom had forgotten how big they were, their bodies solid muscle, their flesh a dull greenish brown, their faces sharp and angular. Some had horns spiralling out of their skulls, around which their matted hair was wrapped.

Arthur ran silently, his sword held before him. Tom followed hesitantly, his sword also drawn. If he was honest, he didn't feel he was needed. Arthur fought with an effortless grace and strength, and his sword looked as if it was an extension of him. He was surefooted and well balanced, and Tom realised clearly, as he hadn't done before, that he was watching Arthur, King of the Britons. He felt a jolt, a sense of unreality that was stronger than anything he'd felt before on this strange journey. The feeling jolted him into the present. He saw everything with an icy clarity: the vast spanning bridges, the high-walled palace of pitted rock, and the cries and shrieks of sprites in the sharp icy air.

Tom ran to Arthur's side and helped distract the sprites, attacking one from behind, unbalancing him so that he fell from the bridge. Tom's heart was pumping, but he didn't have time to feel afraid. When the last sprite was killed, they rolled the bodies off the bridge.

The others joined them and they scanned the upper levels again, but the bridges once more appeared empty, the dark entrances in the rock devoid of life, the spindly trees motionless. After hushed reassurances they pressed on, higher and higher.

There were now eight of them: Arthur, Brenna, Woodsmoke, Finnlugh, Beansprout, and two of the Royal Guard – not many at all, considering what they may find at the top, particularly as Tom and Beansprout had next to no fighting skills. Tom held the sword he had been given, thinking how awkward it felt. He gripped it tighter, wishing his hands didn't feel so sweaty.

Just before they reached the top, Arthur suggested they shared some food to keep them going. He had assumed charge of their small group, and no one thought to question his natural command, not even Finnlugh.

When they had rested, they pressed on to the final bridge and then stopped to assess their position.

They were dizzyingly high. Above them was open sky. The solid walls had gone, and perches lined the latticed walls, beyond which they could see patches of mist that drifted through and hung in the air around them. The wind moaned ceaselessly, carrying the smell of ice and snow. It was freezing, and night was falling. Faint stars began to spark, and a full moon edged above the forest canopy. Below them the bridges criss-crossed back and forth, the floor disappearing into the inky blackness like the bottom of a well. The bridge ahead glowed in the dusk like a ghost road.

Several armed wood sprites stood looking out over the bridge from the opposite side, their dark silhouettes misshapen and deformed.

"They're guarding the throne room," said Brenna.

From the shelter of the doorway, Woodsmoke and the guards exchanged a volley of arrows with the attacking sprites. Eventually the return fire stopped and Arthur led way across the bridge. The anteroom was empty except for their lifeless bodies.

"Useless brutes," Finnlugh said, kicking one as he strode past.

Arthur paid them greater attention, checking to ensure they were all dead.

Beansprout gingerly stepped over them. "It's so eerie here."

Woodsmoke nodded. "I have heard much about this place, but still, this is not what I was expecting."

"Are they all dead? The court, I mean."

"I don't know." He shrugged, looking a little lost.

Finnlugh coughed impatiently. "Finished?"

Woodsmoke bristled with annoyance, but Tom answered, "What now?"

"Now we find my brother and regain the jewel that is rightfully mine."

"Are you prepared for what we'll find in there, Finnlugh?" Arthur asked.

"No. Are you?" Finnlugh asked pointedly.

Arthur ignored him and turned to Brenna. "Do you think the Queen is in there?"

"No. She would have made her presence felt," she said grimly.

"Well then, Finnlugh, the show is yours. Just ensure you do not put anyone here in danger. Or you'll answer to me."

The throne room was guarded by huge double doors of burnished rock and wood. They stood listening for a few seconds, but it was deathly quiet. Arthur turned the handle and pushed open the door.

The throne room was a large square wilderness of cold stone. It was surrounded on three sides by high sheer rocks, and above, it was open to the sky. The fourth side, directly opposite the doors, was edged with a low balustrade, beyond which the sky stretched pitilessly. The floor was of smooth stone, and tall square pillars ran like sentries down either side, creating a ceremonial path to the throne at the far side of the room.

The throne was carved from black granite, and it seemed to suck what little light was left into itself. Crouched in the seat, looking small and insignificant, was the Duke of Craven.

He was focused entirely on a small glowing object in his hands. It gave off a cold blue light, flashing occasionally as he turned it. Before the others could even think, Finnlugh swept his hand to the right and the jewel flew from the Duke's grasp, clattering into the wall and then to the floor.

"Tom, get the jewel!" ordered Finnlugh.

The Duke jerked upright, but before he could react, Finnlugh made a pulling gesture. There was an enormous crack, which echoed off the sheer walls, and the throne began to grate across the floor towards them, the grinding of rock against rock sounding like a wounded animal.

The Duke looked up and smirked, extending his own hands as he did so. The floor rocked with what felt like a wave, knocking the others onto their knees. Only Finnlugh remained standing, his gaze fixed intently on his brother, muttering under his breath, his arm outstretched and his hand palm up.

The noise of the grating stone was almost unbearable. Tom pressed his hands to his ears, but unlike the others, who were edging back beyond the entrance, Tom ran towards the jewel, glowing faintly in the distance.

Finnlugh and the Duke were locked together with fierce intensity. Shards of rock began to fly off the throne, shattering against the surrounding walls and cutting and scratching the others as they retreated. Tom tried to protect his head and eyes and focused only on the jewel. The floor continued to jolt, and Tom ran and fell, and ran and fell.

The others ran back through the open doorway, diving for cover either side of the entrance.

Just as Tom was closing on the jewel, the floor's motion changed. For a moment he thought the floor was dissolving, then he realised it was a shallow pool of water – the violent jolting had caused the water in the pool to slosh across the stone floor. He skidded in the wetness until he finally fell in front of the glowing jewel, and clasped it within his hands.

Tom looked back towards the Prince, but saw only monstrous shadows within a whirling cloud of rocky flints. Moonlight fell on the hall, casting slanting shadows from the pillars, turning the hall into a prison of barred light. The floor continued to buck, and shale started to slip and slither down the walls, forming rivers of rock.

Tom staggered back towards the Prince, wondering how he was going to get the jewel to him as his attention was so fully focused on the Duke. Tom's feet snagged on rock and he stumbled; shale stung his face and he felt blood trickle down his cheeks. Finnlugh saw him and extended his right hand. The wind that now whirled around them meant that Tom could get no closer, so he threw the jewel towards Finnlugh's outstretched hand, hoping it would find a way through the tornado of rock. Finnlugh's break in concentration caused the Duke to push back and Finnlugh staggered, giving the Duke time to turn to Tom, sending a pulse of energy so strong that it threw him back against the wall in the centre of the hall. He dropped like a rag doll into the shale at its base. But it was as if the jewel had been summoned to Finnlugh, and it snapped into his hand with a sound like a thunderclap.

The Duke howled, "No!"

"I told you I would find you and take back my jewel!" Finnlugh shouted. "Surrender while you can."

"Never – you waste your power. It is pointless you having it!"

As the jewel connected to the Prince, it started to swell with light until it encompassed Finnlugh and blinded his brother. An enormous pulse of energy hit the Duke and he rose high into the air before slamming to the floor, motionless.

Finnlugh seemed to shrink, and the jewel pulsed in his hand like a purring cat. He stumbled over to where the Duke lay and stood looking at him in silence, before sinking on to the floor next to his brother's broken but still moving body.

Tom sat rubbing the back of his head. There was a

large lump on it, and bits of flint were lodged in his hair. And he ached all over. The wind had dropped, and now all that disturbed the silence was the trickle of shale.

Arthur stepped through the doorway, followed by the others. He stood next to Finnlugh and said, "You couldn't kill him, then?"

But Finnlugh didn't answer. Arthur continued to watch the twitching form of the Duke.

18　The Old Enemy

Tom sat gazing numbly into the shallow pool of water in front of him. He was too tired to lift his head and instead gazed at the moon's reflection, glittering in the water. The stars were brilliant with diamond light and the sky was thick with them, bathing the hall in a cold white glow.

As Tom sat, half-aware of Arthur's muted footfalls pacing the hall, he saw a gathering patch of darkness in the night sky. The stars started to wink out in ever-increasing numbers, until it seemed something was swallowing them. An arch of shadow cut into the moon, growing bigger. What the hell? It looked like wings, but …

A screech pierced his ears and he looked up to see a vast winged figure fly over the hall. He heard the panic in Brenna's voice as she cried out, "The Queen!"

The black shape wheeled overhead in ever-decreasing circles, until the Queen landed with a shake of her immense wings.

The moonlight cast the Queen's features into sharp lines. Her long oval face was framed by straight black hair that swept past her shoulders and down her back. She was semi-human in form, her legs ending in talons that clattered on the floor, her arms at her side, a cruel jagged knife in one hand. Wings spread from either shoulder, spanning at least five metres, raising and flexing as she strode forward towards her shattered throne. Her eyes were dark black beads that glittered in the half light.

"Brenna," her voice rasped, "it's been too long. I'm so glad you're back. I've been searching for you, and the others. They think they can hide from me, but they can't hide forever. Come into the light, I want to see you."

Brenna moved forward, as if under a spell. Her feet dragged and she clenched her fists, but she was drawn irresistibly onwards until she stepped out of the shadows of the pillars and into a bright patch of moonlight.

"Did you really think you could come here, and that I would allow you to leave?" asked the Queen.

"What did you do to them?" Brenna said, her voice hoarse. "Did you do all this? Did you kill your own people? Your family?"

"They betrayed me! They refused to do as I asked and then tried to depose me. How could I tolerate that?" Her voice rose higher as her anger increased. "Then they abandoned me and the palace. They left me. Me! Fled into the forest. They all left me!" She paused, and stepped forward into the light, her voice now low and dangerous, "And you. You left me years ago, without asking permission."

"You betrayed me, remember? You killed my parents."

"It was a fit punishment for the crime. Treason is an ugly thing."

Arthur remained in the shadows, but his voice rang out. "And you know all about treason, don't you?"

The Queen turned abruptly, trying to find the source of the voice. "Who is that?"

"But I'm so upset. You don't recognise me? I know you. I would recognise that voice anywhere."

She paused, bewildered. "I know who you sound like, but you can't possibly be …"

Arthur had circled behind her, and he called out, "Oh, but I can."

She whirled round in an effort to see him. "But you are dead. You fell in battle."

"As should you be, Morgan. You live well beyond your lifespan."

She gave a cackling laugh. "This world offers many benefits. I could not stay in our world. Others came looking for me. So I made the crossing permanently, to my other home."

Arthur continued to hide in the blackest shadows, pacing silently out of view, leading her away from Brenna.

"So while I have been sleeping," he said, "you have been meddling and destroying – again."

Her claws clattered on the stone as she stepped towards his voice. "I was going to live quietly here in the forest, but … you know me, Arthur."

"Yes I do."

Arthur remained stubbornly hidden from view, fighting for time.

"And you?" she asked. "How are you here?"

"Vivian wished it. But enough of me. You look different. What happened?"

She flexed her wings self-consciously, and for a second Tom sensed regret in her tone. "I had hoped my change in appearance would help me fit in, but things were not as I intended. Magic can be tricky." She tilted her head to one side and looked across to where Finnlugh was slumped with the jewel pulsing softly in his hands.

"I think you've done enough damage here." Arthur

stepped out of the shadows, unexpectedly close to the Queen, and with a flash plunged Excalibur deep into her side.

She screeched and moved swiftly, hurling Arthur backwards with her wing. "You aren't stronger than me any more, Arthur," she said, laughing. "Although Vivian obviously thinks so."

With barely a pause, Arthur rolled forward, slashing Excalibur towards her legs. Taking advantage of the distraction, Woodsmoke released a volley of arrows and the guards rushed in with their swords raised. The arrows bounced off the Queen's wings and onto the floor, and as the guards stepped within her reach she slashed at one with her jagged knife and smashed the other with her powerful wings. The first guard collapsed in a pool of blood and the other was swept over the parapet into the void below. As if to taunt them, she then rose effortlessly out of reach. The wound in her side poured with blood, but it didn't seem to be holding her back.

She landed close to Brenna, calling out, "Try as hard as you like, you can't save Brenna!"

All this time Tom had remained stranded halfway down the throne room, unable to move, where the Duke's blast had thrown him. Beansprout had tried to help Brenna, but the Queen's magic was preventing Brenna from moving.

The Queen was not far from Tom now. He could make out her sharp cruel features and powerful form, and her evil seemed to fill the air.

At some unheard command, Brenna screamed and fell to her knees, her shoulders beginning to tear as wings forced their way out. The air became thick and sticky.

Tom was aware of movement beyond Brenna, and

hoped Finnlugh was doing something. Arrows winged through the air, but fell short of the Queen. Brenna continued her terrifying screams as Arthur ran towards the Queen, his sword raised, but with a wave of her hand the air around him seemed to solidify and he stopped as if turned to stone.

The Queen turned back to Brenna. "I shall put you on these walls; a fine decoration for my hall. And then I shall put Arthur next to you."

Tom couldn't let this happen. But the Queen was so powerful – what could he possibly do? As water lapped gently in the pool in front of him, he remembered the small shell the Emperor had pressed on him before leaving. He pulled it from his pocket and tried to remember what he was supposed do with it. Something about throwing it in water in times of trouble? That seemed too easy. But with Brenna now writhing on the floor and the Queen advancing, he needed to act, not think.

The Queen was standing close to the pool. He threw the shell, and it landed with a splash in the water, ripples spreading outwards. But instead of becoming weaker, the ripples grew stronger, gaining in height and intensity until they broke across the floor of the hall. The Queen hesitated as the water started to froth and boil, and as she paused, thick grasping tentacles whipped upwards out of the pool, followed by a large horny head covered in dozens of round flat eyes. The tentacles grabbed the Queen, enveloping her in their suckered grasp. She screeched and tried to pull free, but the beast had already crushed her wings.

Tom saw her knife rise and fall, but it slashed uselessly. He heard her wings tear as she struggled, and her screams filled the air.

Brenna had now collapsed, seemingly unconscious. Arthur, released from the spell, ran towards the Queen, slashing and parrying, but the tentacles lashing and whipping the air prevented him from reaching her.

Woodsmoke and Beansprout raced to Brenna's side and dragged her to safety.

Tom was too close to the Queen and the tentacled creature. He pushed backwards, hoping to bury himself in the shale. Incredibly, the wounded Queen seemed to be freeing herself. Arthur was caught by a flailing tentacle and thrown against the wall opposite Tom. They could only watch in horror as the Queen wrestled with increasing strength.

Finnlugh rose to his feet. He looked exhausted, but stepping over his brother he strode purposefully to the edge of the pool. He raised his hand and released the power of the jewel. Again its light grew and expanded, and this time Finnlugh grew with it until he was as tall as the pillars, blazing with an unearthly brilliance.

"Hold on tight!" Finnlugh shouted as lightning whipped from the jewel and across the hall.

With an immense crack, a huge rent opened in the sky above the throne room. Tom felt as if he'd been plunged into the centre of the universe. He could see galaxies and planets swirling in reds, greens and blues. They hung above him like fruit; it was as if he could pluck one and take a bite; as if he could step right off this planet and onto one of them. He could almost taste the cosmic dust that glittered in swathes in the vastness of space. Then, with a stab of fear, he realised he couldn't breathe. His lungs heaved and he started to rise into the air. He lunged at the closest pillar and gripped tightly, willing himself not to pass out. He saw

Arthur do the same before he was blocked from view.

The tentacled creature was wrapped tightly around the Queen, and together they rose into the air. Still writhing, they were sucked into the immensity of the universe. Light seemed to be leaking from their every pore, and Tom's last glimpse of the Queen was of one wing breaking free, every tiny feather illuminated by the light beyond it. There was a roar and a shriek, and then silence. The night sky returned and Tom could breathe again.

Tom released the pillar and slumped back to the floor. Finnlugh shrank and collapsed. Tom looked beyond him and realised with a jolt that the Duke had disappeared. He sat up. "Finnlugh, your brother, he's ..."

But before he could finish his sentence, Arthur interrupted. "Tom," he said, shaking his head and pointing upwards.

"You mean–" Tom couldn't finish the sentence.

"Yes."

Tom sighed and looked over at Finnlugh, lying where he'd fallen. After all that, his brother was gone.

He roused himself. What of Beansprout, Woodsmoke and Brenna? How were they? He was about to launch himself to his feet when he saw the doors to the throne room open and Woodsmoke peering through. "All right in there?"

"Just about," Tom said. But he really wasn't sure if any of them would be, ever again.

19 Legacies and Choices

It was a long night for Tom and the others, perched high above the forest. They crossed to the far side of the bridge and made themselves comfortable in the rooms around the stairway. Arthur gathered wood and made a fire at the start of each bridge, to keep away anything else that might have been lurking in the dark. The flames burned bright and high and took the chill off the air. They gathered blankets and sat round the lower fire, not wanting to peer across to the battered throne room.

There were large bleeding wounds on Brenna's shoulders, caused by the forced expansion of her wings, and an exhausted Finnlugh used the jewel to heal them. The scars were red and sore, but her pain was eased.

Nobody felt like talking, and they lay by the fire and fell into a light sleep, Tom haunted by dreams of death.

The next morning they walked out of the palace and down the ridged cliff face, pausing frequently to rest. The thick syrupy air of strong magic had gone, but the forest still seemed to bristle around them with a watchful intensity. Their mood was grim and they mostly walked in silence. When they entered the camp it was with an air of mourning.

"Well thank the Gods, you're all still alive! It's been a horrible night," Jack said, welcoming them with relief.

"You should thank Finnlugh, he was the one who saved us. It was nothing to do with Gods," Tom said.

Jack carried on regardless. "That smell caused by the Duchess's spell was so awful I thought I'd be sick. The wolves came and howled round us for hours, which really upset the horses, and then we saw the lightning shoot from the top of that rock and I nearly had a heart attack."

"I think we all nearly had a heart attack, Granddad," Tom sighed. "At least the smell's gone now," he added reassuringly.

Jack rolled his eyes. "She lifted it at sunrise," he said. "She's a funny old bird, Tom!"

"Not half as bad as the funny old bird we met," Tom grumbled.

Jack burst out laughing. "Good to see you still have your sense of humour."

Tom turned to Finnlugh. "I'm sorry about your brother."

Finnlugh sighed. "I was furious with him, but I didn't want that to happen."

Tom hesitated, wondering what else to say, but Beansprout interrupted. "Well, you shouldn't blame yourself. You did the only thing you could. You saved everyone else."

Finnlugh smiled and patted her arm. "Probably the most good I've done in a long time. However, I do seem to have deprived the forest of its Queen."

"I have the feeling they're not going to miss her much."

"But they need someone," he said.

Woodsmoke interrupted them. "You fancy the job, Finnlugh?"

"Why? Do you?"

"Always so funny," Woodsmoke muttered.

"But shouldn't it be a surviving member of the royal

family? As in someone related to Queen Gavina, or Morgan, or whatever her name is? Was?" Beansprout asked.

Woodsmoke and Finnlugh looked at each other and then over at Brenna, who stood grooming her horse, her movements stiff and awkward.

"Is she related? I mean really related?" Finnlugh asked, the ghost of a smile crossing his face.

"You should probably ask her yourself," Woodsmoke said.

Tom sat facing the fire, staring into its roaring heart as if the answer to every question could be found there. Arthur sat next to him and started to polish his sword. "You look deep in thought, Tom."

"I'm wondering what will happen now."

"What do you want to happen?"

"I have no idea. I suppose I should go home, back to the real world."

"This is a real world."

"Now you sound like Beansprout."

"Really? I've always thought she talked a lot of sense."

Tom sighed. "So what are you going to do?"

"I have no idea. I might go travelling. I want to see more of this new world I'm living in."

"I forgot that you didn't come from here. You're such a legend it seems impossible that you ever really existed in our world. In fact there's nothing to prove you did. It's all just stories."

The light glinted along Excalibur as Arthur cleaned it. "Well I can assure you it was very real. I lived a whole lifetime. It was only yesterday to me, Tom. One day I died and then you woke me here, albeit a younger version of myself than when I died."

"Do you actually remember dying?" asked Tom. "Sorry, is that a gruesome question?" he added, stricken.

Fortunately, Arthur laughed. "No. I remember being injured and feeling this searing pain, like fire, through my side." He gripped his left side as if to remind himself. "I'd been fighting, and I knew it would probably be my last fight, but even so …" He paused and his voice dropped. "There was smoke everywhere, thick and choking as if the camp were on fire, and beneath that was the smell of blood. Sweat was stinging my eyes so that I could hardly see, and I was absolutely bone weary and full of sorrow and regret. And there was a lot of shouting, and the horses were screaming; I remember the thudding of their hooves."

For a second Tom was lost in Arthur's memories, as if he could see it all unfolding around him. "And then?"

"Blackness. Nothingness. No – sometimes there were strange dreams, like being at the bottom of a pool looking up through the murky depths. But I think those came later. Oh, I don't know. Mostly nothing, until you woke me and I rolled out onto the floor of that cave, wondering where I was."

"Did you know about Merlin's deal? That you wouldn't die?"

"Not really. I knew there was something, but not what, and to be honest I didn't care. I had other worries. And I trusted Merlin."

"Do you wish I hadn't woken you?"

"And miss all this? Not many people get two lives, Tom. I should enjoy it while it lasts."

It was evening, and they were all seated around the fire

talking quietly when there was a flurry of activity at the edge of the camp. Finnlugh's guards shouted, and they heard muffled responses. Finnlugh and Arthur leapt to their feet, but Brenna was quickest. She ran to the guards, and after a brief explanation they drew back to let a small group of men and women enter the camp. Brenna hugged them all, and after a few brief words they followed her to the fire.

"They are members of the court," she explained. "Old friends I feared were dead." She turned to them. "Come and join us, have some food."

They were an assortment of the young and old, and all looked weary, although they smiled with relief once they had sat and examined everyone – as closely as everyone looked at them.

"So tell me, are others alive?" asked Brenna, sitting close to them.

"Yes, we are not the only ones. We've been hiding in remote parts of Aeriken for months, some longer than others. But first, is it true? Is she dead?"

"Yes, Finnlugh came to the rescue," Brenna said, pointing him out. "He blasted her out into the universe."

"Indeed," Finnlugh said. "She's somewhere up there, wrestling with a giant sea creature until the end of time."

"That's quite some trick," said one of the younger women, looking worried.

"Don't worry, it exhausts me too much to do it often. But it is impressive," he smirked. The Starlight Jewel was now on a long silver chain around his neck, although buried beneath his clothes, out of sight.

Tom half listened as he gazed into the fire, hearing about others who had fled the Queen's wrath, and her increasing insanity. He was thinking of going to bed when a question grabbed his attention. "So will you stay, Brenna, and help us to bury our dead? And lead us?"

Everyone fell quiet, waiting for Brenna's response. She stared into the fire for a long time, and eventually Woodsmoke said softly, "Brenna?"

She looked at him and then at the others. "I'll stay to help bury our dead, but then I leave. I cannot stay here. It is a place of death. I'll rejoin Woodsmoke and live there. That's my home now."

The oldest man in the group spoke. "But the whole court should move. We would follow you."

"No! I don't want that." She shook her head. "I'm sorry, but that's the way I feel. And actually, I really don't think you need a king or a queen. But I will stay for a while."

"I'll stay too," Woodsmoke said. "I'll help however I can."

"No. It's our job, not yours. But thank you." Brenna gave him the ghost of a smile.

"So," Finnlugh said, "you are the heir?"

"I suppose I am. The Queen was my grandmother. And I hated her."

The last sentence fell awkwardly, and it was Beansprout who broke the silence. "I'm so sorry, Brenna. This is awful. We will all leave tomorrow to let you grieve." She rose and hugged a surprised Brenna. Tom marvelled at Beansprout – she always said the right thing.

The next morning they packed up the camp and said their goodbyes.

"You know you're welcome at any time," Fahey said to Brenna. "It's your home and I'll miss you."

"And you're the sweetest man and I'll miss you too,"

she said, tears in her eyes.

Brenna hugged Tom, Beansprout and Jack, and even Finnlugh. The Duchess merely nodded. "I wish you luck, my dear," was her only comment.

Woodsmoke was less sweet. "You'd better not stay here! This place smells of death. And the wood sprites, they'll be back!"

"We'll be fine! Now stop moaning and go. I'll see you in a few months."

Woodsmoke hesitated, but Brenna persisted. "Go! Please Woodsmoke!" He finally relented and got on his horse.

They nudged their horses and moved off into the forest, leaving Brenna and her friends in the clearing.

"So, what are we going to do?" Tom asked Beansprout.

"I've told you, I'm staying."

"To do what?"

"I don't know, Tom! Do I have to have a plan?"

This was an extension of a long argument that had started on their way back to Woodsmoke's home. They were now only days away, and it seemed as if they had been travelling forever. Aeriken was enormous and ancient, and they had only recently passed the huge stone hawk statues that marked the boundary between Aeriken and Vanishing Wood. Tom couldn't work out how long it had been since they first arrived.

Jack interrupted. "You should both go. You have your whole lives ahead of you. You belong in your own world."

"You have no right to deliver that speech!" said Tom, rounding on him angrily.

"I have every right – I'm your grandfather!"

"Don't you want us here?"

"I didn't think you wanted to be here. Do you know how contrary you are, Tom?" Jack stared angrily back at him. "And of course I want you to stay. It's nice to have my family here. But I'm not going home," he added, preventing any further questions on that. "I'm an old man there, and here – well, I'm less old."

"Don't you care that Mum and Dad have split up?"

"Of course I care, Tom! But my going back wouldn't change anything. They'd still be split up, it's been inevitable for years. And you shouldn't let it affect you. It has nothing to do with you; what you have or haven't done. It's life, and you should get on with yours. Finish school, travel, enjoy yourself."

Jack paused, looking at Tom's mutinous expression. "Just think about the things you've done here. The things you've seen! You're not a child any more."

Arthur joined in. "If life is unsatisfactory, stay here. It sounds like you'd have as much family here as you did there – including me, in case you'd forgotten."

Finnlugh interrupted them all. "You speak as if there was only one choice. You could stay for as long as you wanted, and then go when you were ready."

Tom fell silent. What if he left and then realised he'd made a mistake, and found he could never come back. What then?

A peculiar mood had settled over them all. Although they'd known each other for only a short time, they were reluctant to part. Fahey had been badgering them for information, cheerful in the knowledge he had great tales to create and tell. He and Jack had already arranged to visit Finnlugh's under-palace. Arthur had accepted an invitation to stay at Vanishing Hall, but was planning to travel onwards after a short stay. Beansprout and Tom had also been invited, and Beansprout had accepted immediately.

Tom still wanted to leave. He couldn't explain this need to himself, other than that he somehow felt he should stick to his original intent, which had been to find his grandfather and return home. His questions had been answered, and he felt reassured, if annoyed. He and Jack had made their peace, and he understood Jack's reasons for staying. But he still felt abandoned, and therefore couldn't bring himself to stay too. Now he'd made up his mind, he wanted to leave as quickly as possible.

It was dawn on the outskirts of the wood around Vanishing Hall, and Finnlugh, the Duchess, and the remaining Royal Guard were leaving. Finnlugh shook Tom's hand. "Any time you need anything, just ask."

"That would be a bit difficult from so far away. But thanks. I may see you again."

"And you, dear lady, gentlemen, I shall see you soon." He kissed Beansprout on the cheek, shook hands with the others and then, with a flash of silver and a thudding of hooves, they were gone.

Jack's and Fahey's goodbyes were muted and sad. "I may never see you again, Tom," said Jack, smiling, "but I know you'll be OK." He was unable to hide the small tear that loitered in the corner of his eye. "I can't come to the tower, it will be too much," he said, his voice starting to thicken.

Tom nodded, feeling a little choked and squashing a slight sense of regret. As he shook hands with Fahey, he discovered that his resentment towards his grandfather's friend also seemed to have vanished.

Woodsmoke, Arthur and Beansprout accompanied Tom as they set off back to the doorways.

"I have never heard of these doorways, or seen them," Arthur said. "In my time we crossed by magic through mists and shadows, at dawn or dusk."

"It's only a few hours' ride," Woodsmoke said, "and you'll probably recognise the place."

"What do you mean?" asked Beansprout.

"You'll see."

Slowly emerging through the trees, they saw a large round tower. It was considerably more intact than Mishap Folly. The walls were solid, not crumbling, and it had a door, but the main difference was the long, low, stone building attached to it, with windows and a chimney.

Tom and Beansprout walked towards the tower, mystified.

"The man who built it somehow managed to cross here, and the tower he built on your side appeared here too."

"And where is he?" Tom asked. "Dead, I presume?"

"Oh no. He's around, somewhere. Probably hunting. Sometimes he goes to the village. Anyway, the doorways remain the same, but the entrance here isn't blocked."

Moving to the side of the tower they saw an entrance leading underground. They followed it downwards into a large cave, where four large, stone, arched doorways stood in the centre of the space. The entrances were identical to those they had crossed through, the spaces filled with darkness. They stood before them, and Tom recognised Earth's portal immediately. There were no strange creatures etched in the stone, only images of men and women, a stag's head, and forests.

"Are you sure you want to go, Tom?" Beansprout searched his face carefully, as if he was hiding something.

Now he was here, he really wasn't sure, but he couldn't think of a good reason to stay.

"I must admit, Tom, as anxious as I was to get rid of you, I will miss you," Woodsmoke said.

"Well I'm tempted to come with you," said Arthur, "just to see what the place is like after all these years. But there are things I must see here first. And I've decided to visit Vivian. I think we have lots to talk about."

"Will you ever come back, Beansprout?" Tom asked.

"I'm not sure. Probably. What if we say we'll cross in a year from now?"

"Yes, we'll come, see how you are. See if you want to return," Woodsmoke said.

"See if I want to stay!" Beansprout added.

"Yes, OK." Tom nodded. "The time may be different there, but I'll be at the cottage or thereabouts."

"What will you tell my mother?"

"What do you want me to tell her?"

"Tell her I'm fine, and I'm safe, and I'm staying with Granddad. The rest is up to you."

"OK." Tom looked around for the last time, at his friends, at the cave, at the doorways, and took a deep breath. He gave them a brief hug. "No goodbyes!" Turning, he stood in front of Earth's doorway then stepped through.

He felt the weightlessness, the sensation of falling, and the now-familiar jolt, as the ground appeared beneath him. He felt warm earth and sunshine. Looking up he found himself on the bank opposite his grandfather's house. It was summer. The trees were thick with dark green leaves and the garden was choked with flowers.

He was home.

Read on for an excerpt of Twice Born, book 2 in Tom's Arthurian Legacy.

T. J. GREEN

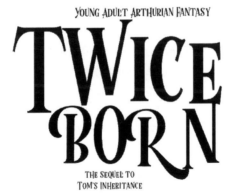

YOUNG ADULT ARTHURIAN FANTASY

TWICE BORN

THE SEQUEL TO
TOM'S INHERITANCE

3 The Hollow Bole- Excerpt

Tom and the others rode into Holloways Meet on a hot dusty afternoon. The road broadened and dipped until they reached a large archway formed by thick interlaced branches. Beyond that, a few small buildings began to appear, built into the high banks of the road. Within a short distance they could hear a steady hum of voices, shouts, laughter and music, and the banks fell back to form a large irregular square dominated by a central group of trees with other Holloways leading into it. It was filled with an assorted collection of beings, young and old, colourful and drab, and the smell of business.

Wooden buildings threaded through the meeting place, some of them perched precariously in branches, others jostling for position on the fields above them, casting deep shadows onto the activities in the centre.

"This place looks busier than ever," Brenna murmured.

"What do people do here?" Tom asked, looking around curiously.

"Many things. I have been told you can buy almost anything here, and travellers use it to stock up on supplies. Consequently, a lot of people pass through so it's particularly useful for finding out information."

"I love it!" Beansprout said, grinning.

"We'd better find Woodsmoke and Arthur.

Woodsmoke said he would try to check into the Quarter Way House," said Brenna. She pointed to a big building with balconies on the far side of the square, built against the bank and onto the field at the top. "It's more expensive than most, but it guarantees a clean bed and good food."

They found Woodsmoke and Arthur sitting in a bar to the side of the main entrance. It was an oasis of calm after the bustle of the square, filled with an assortment of tables and chairs, and screened from the square by thick-limbed climbing plants covered with flowers and a coating of wind-blown dust.

"Well, don't you two look relaxed!" Brenna said, hands on hips.

"The rest of the deserving after a hard day's work!" Woodsmoke said with a smirk as he and Arthur stood to greet them. "Tom – you're here! And you've grown." He walked around the table and grabbed him in a bear hug. "I wasn't sure if I'd ever see you again."

"You have no idea how pleased I am to be back," Tom said, giving Woodsmoke an equally big hug in return.

Tom turned to Arthur, who gripped the top of his arms and stared at him. "You look well, Tom. It's good to have my great-great-great-something-relative here," and he gave him such a crushing hug that Tom struggled for breath.

Now he was reunited with all five of his closest friends in the Other (or anywhere else), he really felt he was back. Unlike Brenna and Beansprout, Arthur and Woodsmoke looked reassuringly the same. Although Tom had grown, they were both still taller than him, Woodsmoke lean and rangy, his longbow propped next to him at the table, and Arthur muscular, Excalibur in its scabbard at his side.

"Let's get more drinks to celebrate," Arthur said, and called to the barman. "Five pints of Red Earth Thunder Ale please!"

As they sat, Beansprout asked, "So how long have you been here?"

"We arrived this morning," Woodsmoke answered, "and thought we needed to recover after our long days on the road." He paused as their ale arrived, and took a long drink as if to emphasise his need to recuperate.

"But," said Arthur, "we think that Nimue stayed at the Hollow Bole – well, Vivian thought she did, apparently it's where she's stayed before. That's where I'll be going soon, to ask a few questions." He looked at Tom. "Do you want to come?"

"Yes," Tom said, spluttering his drink in an effort to answer. "But first tell me what happened with Vivian."

"Ah!" Arthur said gazing into his pint, "Vivian. It was very strange to meet her again, after so many years. I felt quite sick seeing that big, bronze, dragon-headed prow gliding out of the mist." He sighed, trying to organise his story. "I met her by the lake, at her request. I'd wanted to contact her, but didn't know how. I thought that standing at the lakeside, yelling into the mist probably wouldn't work," he said with a grin. "But then I had these images enter my dreams, about the standing stones and the lakeside."

"Oh, yes," Tom interrupted, "I've experienced those!"

"So I headed to the lake and within an hour the boat was there, and then almost instantly she was at my side. She looked so old, and yet so young." He looked up at the others as if trying to make them see what he had. "I couldn't believe her hair was white! It used to be a rich dark brown that glinted with red when it caught the sunlight. She had freckles then, all over her nose and cheeks." He shook himself out of his reverie as his friends watched him, fascinated by what he must be remembering. "She asked me if I remembered her sisters, the other priestesses, particularly Nimue, which I did. Nimue helped me rule when Merlin disappeared. Vivian explained that Nimue had vanished on her way to Dragon's Hollow to see Raghnall, the dragon enchanter – whoever he is. She was taking her time, visiting various people along the way. The last time Vivian heard from her was when she was here, at Holloways Meet. It takes about a week to travel to Dragon's Hollow from here, but she never arrived there."

"And how does Vivian know she hasn't arrived?" Beansprout asked.

"Because Raghnall contacted Vivian, by scrying, to find out where Nimue was. Apparently Vivian has been trying to contact her ever since, again by scrying, which is apparently how they communicate long distance. Now Vivian thinks she's being blocked, either by Nimue or someone else."

"What's Nimue like?" Tom asked.

"Oh, she's very different to Vivian. She's small and dark haired, liked a pixie, very pretty. Merlin was infatuated with her," Arthur said thoughtfully. "Vivian is worried that something is wrong, so we've spent the last few weeks trying to track her route, but we've found nothing of interest. It all seems a wild goose chase," he said, finishing his pint. "So, Tom, shall we go? Woodsmoke looks too comfortable to move." He frowned at Woodsmoke, who had his feet up on a chair looking very relaxed.

"It's been a busy few weeks," Woodsmoke said, indignant, "and I'm much older than you are, so I deserve to relax. Besides, I also have news to catch up on," he added, gesturing to Brenna and Beansprout. He waved them off. "Enjoy your afternoon."

Tom and Arthur set off on a slow circuitous route.

"I know I've been here a few months now, Tom, but I still can't get used to the place."

Tom nodded. "I know what you mean."

Strange creatures bustled across the square, some tall, some small, male and female, some part human, part animal. They passed a group of satyrs and felt small by comparison. The satyrs were over seven feet tall, with muscular bodies, the upper half bare-chested, the lower half with the hairy legs of goats. Their hair was thick and coarse, large curling rams' horns protruded from their heads, and their eyes were a disconcerting yellow that made them look belligerent. Tom and Arthur skirted past them, making their way to a row of buildings at the side of the square. These were a mixture of shops, semi-permanent markets, eating places and inns, ranging from the small and shabby to the large and less shabby. Smoke from braziers drifted through the still air. They looked at the wooden signs that hung from the entrances, trying to find the Hollow Bole.

They had been looking for nearly an hour, taking their time drifting through the warren of buildings, before they had any joy. Walking down the start of one of the Holloways, they saw a vast tree to their left, pressing against the bank at its back. There was a narrow cleft in its trunk, above which a small sign announced *The Hollow Bole*. Peering upwards through the leaves they saw small windows scattered along thick and misshapen branches. Ducking to avoid hitting their head on the low entrance, they stepped into a small hall hollowed out of the trunk and followed the narrow spiralling stairs upwards into the gloom. They emerged into a larger hall built into a broad branch overlooking the Holloway and the edge of the square. There were no straight edges anywhere. Instead, the chairs, tables and balcony were an organic swirl of living wood.

A dryad, green skinned and willowy, stepped out of the shadows and said, "Can I help you?"

Thinking they were alone, Tom jumped. Arthur remained a little more composed and said, "I'm looking for an old friend who passed through here, probably a few weeks ago now. Can you confirm if she stayed here?"

"And what do you want with this friend?" the dryad snapped.

"She hasn't arrived where she should have, and I want to find out if anything has happened to her," Arthur said, trying to keep the impatience out of his voice.

The dryad went silent for a moment. "It depends who it is. Her name?"

"Nimue. Our mutual friend Vivian asked me to find her. She's worried."

The dryad was startled. "Nimue? The witch?" She spat out "witch" viciously.

Now Arthur was startled. "Yes, Nimue, one of the priestesses of Avalon. Or *witch*, as you choose to call her."

"They are all witches on Avalon," the dryad replied disdainfully. "Yes, she stayed here for a few days. And then she left. I don't know where," she added, to avoid further questions.

Arthur groaned. "She gave no indication at all of where she might be going?"

"She stays here because we are discreet. We ask no questions of our clients."

"But you know her well? She stays here often I

believe."

"Not often. She travels less frequently now. But yes, I believe she usually stays here. However, I do not know her well. I do not ask questions."

Tom was curious about the word "now", and clearly Arthur was too.

"But she used to travel here more frequently? In the past?" said Arthur.

The dryad was visibly annoyed at the constant questions. "Yes, many years ago. But, I do not see what that has to do with now – and I was not here then."

"So if you weren't here then, how do know she came here?" Arthur persisted.

"Her name appears in our old registers. We are an old establishment. And her reputation precedes her."

Now Arthur was clearly very curious, and he leaned in. "What reputation?"

"As a witch from another world. A meddler in the affairs of others."

"What affairs?"

"Witches meddle with the natural order of nature!" the dryad snapped, now furious. "As a dryad, I am a natural being, born of the earth and all her darkest mysteries. Witches plunder that knowledge! They have no respect for natural laws. How do *you* know her?"

Arthur looked uncomfortable and decided not to answer that. "I am just an old friend who cares for her safety. I am sorry to have taken so much of your time. If you're sure you don't remember anything else?"

"Nothing."

"Just one more question. Did she ever stay here with anyone else?"

"Yes. The greatest meddler of them all – Merlin."
With that, she stepped back into the shadows and melted
into the tree trunk, becoming invisible and unreachable.

Twice Born is on sale now

Author's Note

All authors love reviews. They're important because they help drive sales and promotions, so please leave a review on either Amazon or Goodreads – or another retailer of your choice! Your review is much appreciated.

If you'd like to read more of my writing, please join my mailing list by visiting www.tjgreen.nz. You can get a free short story called *Jack's Encounter*, describing how Jack met Fahey – a longer version of the prologue in *Tom's Inheritance* – by subscribing to my newsletter. You'll also get a FREE copy of *Excalibur Rises*, a short story prequel.

You will also receive free character sheets on all of my main characters in White Haven Witches, my urban fantasy series - exclusive to my email list!

By staying on my mailing list you'll receive free excerpts of my new books, as well as short stories and news of giveaways. I'll also be sharing information about other books in this genre you might enjoy.

To get your FREE short story please visit my website
http://www.tjgreen.nz

I look forward to you joining my readers' group.

Acknowledgements

This book has been a long time in the making. Thanks to Jason and my mother, Hazel, for their endless encouragement and support.

Thanks also to Jason, Mom, Terri and Jo, for their enthusiastic response to early drafts of the manuscript and their helpful suggestions as to plot and characterisation. Thanks to Jade for the proofread. Many other friends and family have been curious about and supportive of my endeavours, so thanks to all of you too. You were very patient.

I have been fortunate enough to be part of a writing group who have given time and thought to my work in progress. Their suggestions have been great, and I wish them luck with their projects.

Big thanks to Sue Copsey, my editor, for her great observations, suggestions and skilled editing, and lots of other great advice on everything else involved in publishing. Hopefully she'll want to do this again.

And thanks also to all the writers who have gone before me in exploring and creating the myths and legends of King Arthur.

I must also thank the very real Tom, who gave me the inspiration for starting the short story that turned into Tom's Inheritance. He's a little too young to read it now, but I hope he enjoys it when he's older.

About the author

T.J. Green grew up in England and now lives in the Hutt Valley, near Wellington, New Zealand, with her partner Jason, and her cats Sacha and Leia. When she's not writing, she enjoys reading, gardening, shopping and yoga.

In a previous life she's been a singer in a band, and has done some acting with a theatre company – both of which were lots of fun. On occasions she and a few friends make short films, which begs the question, where are the book trailers? Coming soon …

Other ongoing projects include a book set in the real world (whatever that is) – but there will be unusual things happening.

Website: http://www.tjgreen.nz
Facebook: https://www.facebook.com/tjgreenauthor/
Twitter: https://twitter.com/tjay_green
Pinterest: https://nz.pinterest.com/mount0live/my-books-and-writing/
Goodreads: https://www.goodreads.com/author/show/15099365.T_J_Green
Instagram: https://www.instagram.com/mountolivepublishing/

BookBub: https://www.bookbub.com/authors/tj-green

Amazon:
https://www.amazon.com/TJ-Green/e/B01D7V8LJK/

Printed in Great Britain
by Amazon